# Game of
# CLONES

J-FICTION

ALSO BY M.E. CASTLE

*Popular Clone*
*Cloneward Bound*


OTHER EGMONT PUBLISHING BOOKS
YOU MAY ENJOY

*Guinea Dog*
by Patrick Jennings

*My Homework Ate My Homework*
by Patrick Jennings

*How to Grow Up and Rule the World*
by Vordak the Incomprehensible

# Game of CLONES

## THE CLONE CHRONICLES #3

### M.E. CASTLE

EGMONT
Publishing

New York

# EGMONT

*We bring stories to life*

First published by Egmont USA, 2014
This paperback edition published by Egmont Publishing, 2015
443 Park Avenue South, Suite 806
New York, NY 10016

1 3 5 7 9 8 6 4 2

www.egmontusa.com
www.theclonechronicles.com

THE LIBRARY OF CONGRESS HAS CATALOGED THE
HARDCOVER EDITION AS FOLLOWS:

Castle, M.E.
Game of clones /M/E. Castle.
pages cm – (The Clone Chronicles ; #3)
Summary: Twelve-year-old Fisher Bas and the clone he created try to prevent a
mad scientist and his evil clone brother from trying to take over the world through
a behavior-altering television program.
ISBN 978-1-60684-234-8 (hardcover) -- ISBN 978-1-60684-472-4 (ebook)
[1. Cloning—Fiction. 2. Reality television programs—Fiction. 3. Scientists—Fiction. 4. Bullies—Fiction. 5. Middle Schools—Fiction. 6. Schools—Fiction]
I. Title.
PZ7.C2687337Gam 2014
[Fic]--dc23
2013018266

Paperback ISBN 978-1-60684-538-7

Printed in the United States of America

*For my mother,*
*Who has given me love and care in infinite supply*
*And has never explicitly voiced a wish*
*To return me to the thrift store*
*Where I was purchased.*

# Game of
# CLONES

# ≋ CHAPTER 1 ≋

Scientists aren't the people who always have good ideas. They're the people whose bad ideas make the biggest explosions.　　　　　—Fisher Bas, Personal Notes

"The goat ate my pants."

"Are you sure?"

"I was wearing them when I went to sleep. I woke up with a satisfied goat staring down at me, and no pants. Is that enough evidence for you?"

Thus began episode six of the new reality TV sensation *Family Feudalism*, featuring none other than long-separated brothers Martin and Harold Granger, better known to Fisher as Dr. Devilish and Dr. X.

Dr. X, a short and spindly man with a hawkish nose, tried to shoo the goat out of the room while his brother, Dr. Devilish, continued to lament.

"I'll have to spin a new pair from wool," Dr. Devilish said. He was much larger than his older brother, with a jawline that could cut glass, and perfectly straight hair that was almost as dense as the head it sat on. He adjusted his beige cotton long johns. "I'm sure they won't be nearly as formfitting—"

"Okay!" said *Family Feudalism*'s host, Terry Trebu-chet, popping into the room in his green, purple, and gold jester's outfit and jangly five-pointed bell hat. The goat turned and stared up at him with wide, unblink-ing eyes. "Are you two ready to overcome today's chal-lenge?"

"Scarcely a month ago," said Dr. X, his eyes drifting upward, as though he were appealing to the heavens, "I was ready to overcome all of humanity. To sweep across the globe with my glorious robot army. To bring the con-tinents and oceans into my domain, an empire to last ten thousand years . . ." His eyes grew misty.

Terry Trebuchet stared uneasily at the camera. "I'll take that as a yes," he said, with a nervous giggle.

Dr. Devilish clapped his brother on the back. "Don't listen to him. You know how my poor, poor brother gets." He pulled an expression of deep sadness. It was terri-bly unconvincing, but then, if he were a good actor, he wouldn't be stuck on a ridiculous medieval-themed real-ity show with his ex–evil overlord brother.

Fisher, who was watching the show on his computer, pushed back from his desk. "This has to be the worst show I've ever seen," he commented to his clone, Two.

Two was a perfect physical copy of Fisher—a small, skinny twelve-year-old boy with short brown hair. The only obvious difference between them was the number of freckles on their noses: Fisher had three, and Two had come up one short.

But considering Fisher had made Two himself in his own bedroom, that detail and Two's left-handedness were pretty minor deviations.

"I just can't believe it," Two said. "Why doesn't Devilish rat out Dr. X? He should be in jail, not on TV. It's been barely a month since Dr. X tried to kill us all. I can't imagine his brother's forgiven him yet." Two carefully inverted his new Onion Detector, which was about the size of a Q-tip. Two hated onions and had invented a tiny reader so that he could surreptitiously be sure there were no onions in his meals—especially if he was about to see Amanda, and breath was a concern. So far, the detector had successfully measured that there were, in fact, onions on Earth. It needed some fine-tuning to be more precise.

"At this point, I think Devilish's career is all he cares about," said Fisher. "Devilish saw an opportunity when Dr. X got deposed by Three. I bet you anything he black-mailed Dr. X into going on the show with him. Knowing Dr. Devilish, I'm sure he can set his personal feelings aside for popularity's sake." Fisher rolled his eyes. Back in Los Angeles, before their last confrontation with Dr. X and his terrifying creation, Three, Fisher and Two had spent plenty of time observing Dr. Devilish. They knew he would do almost anything for fame—including lie for

3

years about scientific credentials. Fisher went on, "It's weird seeing Dr. X like this. No fancy equipment. No fortress. No robots. Just a scared, little man."

Fisher didn't add that seeing Dr. X au naturel reminded him of the Harold Granger Fisher had once known—the middle school biology teacher who had been one of Fisher's only friends.

Fisher pushed the thought out of his mind. Harold Granger had just been an act, a cover story. And so had Dr. X's friendship.

"Speaking of scared," Two said, his eyes still glued to the screen, "you seem a little jumpy yourself."

November was upon them, and that meant it was the night of their school's fall formal. All day, Fisher had felt as if his limbs were filled with a thousand angry hornets. "I've . . . never actually been to a dance," he admitted.

"You'll be fine," Two said. "And if you aren't, you can always hide out in the locker rooms while I have all the fun."

"Gee, thanks," Fisher said, nudging Two's shoulder. They laughed, briefly awakening FP, whose head was inside an empty popcorn bucket. Fisher's little pet pig stirred momentarily before his snoring resumed.

On the show, Terry led the way out of the hut, pointing to a small cart with solid wooden wheels next to a pair of donkeys.

"A crucial part of a medieval peasant's life was taking harvested crops to the market town to sell," Terry said. "To do that, they would use a cart, like this one. Your first challenge is simple. Work together to hitch the donkeys to the cart, then drive it to the wooden post at the other side of this field."

The Grangers looked at the donkeys, at the cart, and at each other.

"You start," they said at the same time.

"No, *you* start," they said at the same time.

"I'm an intellectual titan!" Dr. X said. "I should be organizing the effort and you should provide the brute physical force I require!"

"I'm the TV celebrity!" said Dr. Devilish, planting his hands on his hips. "You should listen to what I say."

"What *you* say??" Dr. X exclaimed. "You were a pretend TV scientist who did a hair gel commercial with a talking cartoon porpoise!"

"Don't you bad-mouth Pasquale Porpoise," said Dr. Devilish. "At least he never tried to *kill me with robots*."

"Gentlemen!" said Terry. "Gentlemen! You've got five minutes. I think you should get to work, yes?"

The Grangers shot one more nasty look at each other, then stalked in silence toward the donkeys.

"Come here, you filthy *Equus asinus* . . . ," Dr. X muttered as he reached for a donkey's head. In response, the donkey shot a hoof straight into his chest, sending him somersaulting backward through the mud. Dr. Devilish's donkey scampered to the other side of the cart.

The Grangers spent most of the five-minute clock chasing the donkeys around in circles.

"That's it!" Dr. X crowed at the top of his lungs. "I will not be subject to this humiliation any longer!" With that, he pulled a device from his pocket and pressed a button. The show's microphones picked up a very faint, high-pitched hum.

Immediately, the donkeys stopped running.

And started dancing. And where donkeys are concerned, the place where running ends and "dancing" begins is a fine and fuzzy line. Before the timer had finished counting off five minutes, the Grangers were diving over a low post fence to get away from the donkey flamenco.

"I recognize that device!" said Fisher, over the sounds of shouting from both the brothers and the host. "I saw it being tested in TechX. On whales."

"Yup. I watched those experiments," added in CURTIS, the artificial intelligence residing in Fisher's computer. CURTIS closed down the video window and immediately opened a new one that featured a simple face module of CURTIS's own invention. It featured a series of slightly different smiley faces that shifted as he talked to

# TECH-X
# KILLER WHALE DEVICE

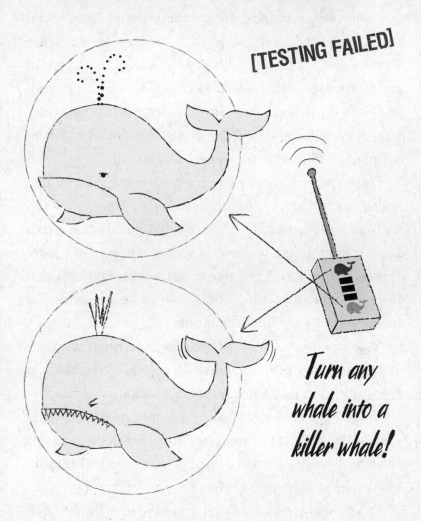

communicate his feelings. Fisher had taken CURTIS out of TechX with him, and the AI had proven to understand human interaction better than he did.

Fisher still struggled to get the hang of most social skills that other kids seemed to possess innately. He found it difficult to deal with problems that didn't involve multipart equations or electron transfer. But he was willing to face his fears now. He'd changed since he'd infiltrated TechX, the pyramid-like fortress that Dr. X had occupied in Palo Alto, to rescue his clone.

Facing such a challenge and near-certain doom had added a little steel to his backbone. And not, CURTIS had once said, because he succeeded, but because he'd been willing to risk failure. He was still scared of a lot of things, but he wasn't paralyzed by them. He never would have attempted tracking down Two in Los Angeles if it hadn't been for the TechX mission.

"It was supposed to make whales into programmable assassins," CURTIS continued. "Instead, it taught them the waltz." The face made a sort of smirk.

"I just can't believe what's happened to Dr. X," said Fisher. "He's one of the smartest and most devious people the world has ever known. And Three knocked him off his throne in a matter of days."

Three was another clone made from Two's DNA (which was, of course, also Fisher's DNA). He had been manufactured by Dr. X to be a drone: a perfect killing machine. And although Fisher, Two, and Three all resembled one another physically, Three was a horribly distorted version of the two brothers—with no morals, scruples, or feelings, and a single driving desire: power. Dr. X had, for once in his life, miscalculated. He believed he could control Three. He had been proven wrong.

"He must have been planning a takeover from the start," Two said grimly.

"I almost feel sorry for Dr. X," Fisher said. Two shot him a look, and he repeated, *"Almost."*

"Fisher?" came his mother's voice as the door opened with no warning. Two dropped to the floor and rolled under the bed like the room had caught a hail of gunfire.

"Oh, hi, Mom!" he said, spinning in place and trying to look as normal and casual as possible.

"Just brought you up some clean laundry," she said, setting down a laundry basket that ordinarily could walk up the stairs by itself, but had been malfunctioning lately. "Looking forward to the dance?"

"Yep," Fisher said. But the reminder sent a twinge of fear through him. "Should be a great time."

His mother smiled and walked out, closing the door behind her.

Two crawled out from under the bed and leaned against a wall. Instantly, Fisher could tell something was the matter. Two's arms were crossed and he was scowling.

"Two?" said Fisher. "What's up?"

"Nothing," Two said, whipping around to face him. "Nothing at all. Why, you ask? Because the world doesn't know I *exist*! So how could anything be wrong? *No one knows I'm even real.*"

"Two," Fisher said cautiously, "we've talked about this. . . ."

"I'm tired of talking," Two cut in. CURTIS's dot eyes moved back and forth nervously between Two and Fisher. The face window closed to give them the illusion of privacy. "You promised me you'd tell the truth weeks ago."

"I know," Fisher said, sighing. "But I just . . . haven't found the right time yet. Or the right way."

"The right time," Two grunted. "The right way."

"It's true," Fisher said. "This is something we need to plan carefully." CURTIS subtly opened the video window again as a preview for the next episode of *Family Feudalism* came on.

"I'm sorry, Fisher. I can't quite make out what you're saying," Two said, stalking to the other side of the room. "All I'm hearing is *bawwk, bawk, bawk, baaaawwwk. . . .*"

"All right," he said, collapsing onto his bed. "You're right. I'm scared. But that's not the reason we should wait."

"Waiting isn't helping us. Look, you said it yourself," Two said, beginning to pace the small room. "Dr. X is one of the smartest and most evil people on Earth, and Three seized power from him in less than a month. Three's more dangerous than even we imagined. He could be anywhere, planning anything, and he's got all the resources Dr. X used to control. We need to get out there and find him!"

"I know, I know," Fisher said. "And we will. Soon." He looked at the clock. Almost 6 P.M. "For tonight, let's just try and have a good time at the fall formal."

"That's another thing," Two said. "You get to go to the formal in a tux while I have to wear *that*." He pointed to a corner of the room, where a multicolored, feathered monster was propped against the wall. The suit had started its life as the Furious Badger, Wompalog Middle School's old mascot. Two had converted it into a double-billed yellow-bellied bilious duck suit to protest the King of Hollywood restaurant's invasion of the ducks' habitat, and the duck had been adopted as the school's new mascot.

"We made a deal," Fisher said, standing up. "I'm the one that's been going to school for the last three weeks—five, if you count the time you spent running around LA—while you were doing whatever you wanted to do. I go to school; I get to go to the formal as me. At least Amanda knows what's going on. She'll understand. I have to keep lying to Veronica."

"You don't *have* to," Two said. "You could tell her about me. You could tell everyone."

"Please let's not get back into this," Fisher said, rubbing his forehead.

Two looked at the DBYBBD costume and frowned. "Fine. But you're the giant clown duck next time."

"There won't be a next time, Two," Fisher said. "I promise."

"Promises, promises," Two muttered.

Fisher and Two brushed their teeth, combed their hair, and donned identical suits. Then Two sighed and climbed into the duck suit. While Fisher walked downstairs and out the front door, Two placed a remote-activated ladder out Fisher's window and slunk around the back.

By the time FP stirred and woke, Two and Fisher were long gone. The little pig pulled his head out of the bucket and looked around, sniffing the air. Then, realizing there was a leftover unpopped kernel in the bucket, he spent the next hour trying to reach it before again passing out in exactly the same position Fisher and Two had left him.

# ≋ CHAPTER 2 ≋

*If everyone does their part just right, a plan will work with-out a hitch. That's why I call my sidekick the Hitch Factory.*
—Vic Daring, Space Scoundrel, *Issue #237*

Wompalog's gym was covered in balloons and painted papier-mâché decorations, reflecting the fall formal's "theme." The dance committee had hit a deadlock, with half the members in favor of one classic theme and half in favor of another. At the last minute, they had decided to compromise. So the theme of the fall formal was Arabian Nights Under the Sea.

There were stands of palm trees with long strips of kelp hanging from them. Spaced around the sides of the gym and on the dance floor were pieces made to look like piles of sand decorated with scorpions, cobras, and star-fish. And hanging above the buffet tables were two camel-seahorse hybrids, like one might find in Mr. Bas's lab.

Fisher and Two walked into the gym as it filled up, bass thudding through the floor. People cheered and pointed at the sight of the duck. Nobody noticed that its shoulders were slumped and its posture sullen.

Amanda Cantrell, in a dark green dress that showed

off her toned shoulders, walked up to Fisher and Two, glanced at Fisher with something that was closer to a stab than a look, and took Two's rubbery, feathered hand. They walked off into the growing crowd. She wasn't pleased with Fisher's choice of costume for Two, but she was never pleased with anything Fisher did, so he was used to it.

Fisher sometimes wondered if Amanda had a lingering distrust of him. When Two had first come to school, she'd developed quite a crush on him—believing that he was simply a new, improved, more confident Fisher.

Eventually, she began to notice the differences between the two boys, though, forcing Fisher to reveal Two's existence to her. He'd also made her swear not to reveal his existence to anyone else, and she clearly resented the fact that her boyfriend was Fisher's deepest secret.

Despite her misgivings, she'd helped him find Two in LA, and fight Dr. X when he had reemerged. He hoped she did trust him, because he had to trust her. She was the only person besides him and the Granger brothers who knew that Two existed. Admittedly, GG McGee and Kevin Keels had seen Fisher and Two together, but they had likely mistaken them for twins. For that matter, Dr. Devilish probably had, too. Fisher wasn't too concerned about them. Together, they had an intellect slightly more impressive than a tulip's.

"Hi, Fisher."

He turned around at the sound of Veronica Greenwich's voice, and his heart instantly responded by rocketing into his throat. She wore a long black dress with a pleated skirt, accented by a silver necklace and earrings. Her wheat-gold hair was swept into an elegant bun.

None of this consciously registered to him, of course. He simply saw the loveliest sight he'd ever seen, and acted accordingly. That is, he opened his mouth to say hello back and only a sound like a tiny leak in a steam pipe emerged.

"Pretty dumb decorations, aren't they?" she said. Without waiting for him to respond, she said, "Dance?"

"Dance . . . ," Fisher said, still having trouble getting his chugging brain up to speed, "with you?"

"No, Fisher, I'm asking on that seahorse-camel's behalf. She was too shy to ask you herself," she said, smiling.

"Oh . . . er . . ."

"Yes, with me! Come on!" She reached out and took his hand, gently pulling him to the middle of the dance floor.

Fisher pretended to stumble as he walked, and struck his left heel sharply against the floor. This activated his newest invention: the iGotRhythm Dynamic Automated Dancing Shoes. His footwear, which appeared to be ordinary black dress shoes, contained sophisticated electronic equipment and powerful magnetic motors. Their built-in microphones could detect even a subtle beat, and the motors in the shoes would then force his feet to move in time to the music and in a style appropriate to the music's tempo and rhythm.

At least, that was what had happened when Fisher had tested the shoes in the solitude of his own room. Here on a crowded, noisy dance floor, they would be put through their first field test.

The first song was slow enough that Fisher could get used to the way that the shoes pulled and pushed at his feet. He took Veronica's right hand in his left and rested his right hand on her hip.

She smiled at him as they moved smoothly along the floor. So far, the shoes were a complete success. His feet moved perfectly with the music and didn't bump into hers once. He hoped the second invention he had brought— a small pocket fireworks display, which he intended to show her in the school's athletic field after the dance was over—worked just as well.

Veronica glanced over Fisher's shoulder.

"I'm kind of surprised that FP isn't here, inhaling the buffet and swimming in the punch bowl," she said with a grin.

"I learned a little bit from the LA trip," Fisher responded easily. Now that his body was moving with grace and fluidity, it was much easier to get his voice under control.

# iGotRhythm
# DYNAMIC AUTOMATED
# DANCING SHOES

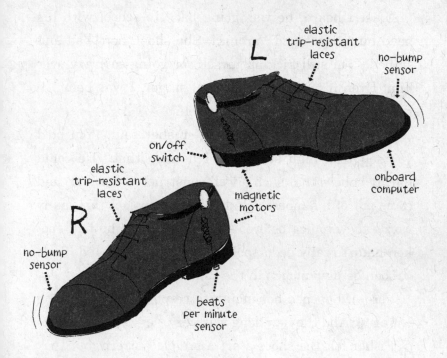

L

elastic
trip-resistant
laces

no-bump
sensor

on/off
switch

elastic
trip-resistant
laces

magnetic
motors

onboard
computer

R

no-bump
sensor

beats
per minute
sensor

"He's no longer invited to parties."

"Good thinking," she said as he carefully attempted to spin her. He succeeded, to his surprise. Veronica giggled.

"So," he said cautiously, "has there been any news on Kevin Keels lately?"

Veronica blushed. She'd gotten caught up in the fervor

surrounding the young pop star. Then someone had leaked a video of Keels actually singing—not just lip-synching while he swiveled across the stage—and that fervor had collapsed like an elephant on toothpick stilts.

"Last I heard, he was going back to school with his head hung low," said Veronica. She shook her head and smiled. "I'm still kicking myself for going so crazy over him. Even if he *had* been a real singer, I was being so ridiculous! I expect better of myself."

"We all do ridiculous things," Fisher said. "You hold yourself to a high standard. I admire that." He could hardly believe that such a well-constructed sentence had come out of his mouth. He had never spoken this many words to Veronica before. And those words he had spoken hadn't really been spoken so much as blurted like a baboon being punched in the stomach.

Veronica opened her mouth to respond when the song changed. And the new song was very, very fast.

Fisher felt the shoes start a simple pattern, but they paused briefly, and he felt a faint click near his left big toe. That meant the onboard (or in-shoe) computer was making a decision.

Unfortunately, that decision turned out to be a blazing tango.

The shoes carved a trail along the floor with Fisher in tow. Fisher could barely hang on to Veronica. They went forward and backward as he took powerful, sharp steps. He led her all around the dance floor, and the other couples parted and stepped back to watch.

He was even able to execute a few turns and spins. When the number ended with a dip, his short arms strained for the leverage to support her as she leaned back, her head a foot from the floor.

Fisher pulled Veronica back upright when the next song began. Sweat beaded and trailed down his forehead as the kids around them clapped.

"Wow, Fisher," Veronica said, out of breath. "I had no idea you were such a dancer."

"I . . . didn't, either," he said. He was totally exhausted but at least he hadn't made an idiot of himself. "I . . . think I'm going to try some of that punch."

Veronica nodded. "I see a friend of mine in the corner. I'm going to say hi. Meet you there?"

Fisher nodded, smiled, and tapped his heel on the floor again. But instead of powering down the motor, the shoes switched to a waltz, and he was forced to execute a little one-two-three, one-two-three off the dance floor. He grabbed a table with both hands and hit his heel harder. This time, the shoes stopped.

He reached the punch and immediately downed three cups of the red-orange concoction before his breathing slowed to normal. He leaned against the wall, searching the crowd for Veronica. The gym was completely packed.

Instead, he saw Two, still wearing the duck costume, climbing up onto the stage next to the DJ. Two wrestled off the mascot head. Fisher dropped his fourth cup of punch and ducked behind the nearby bleachers.

What was Two thinking?!

The DJ tossed Two a mic, then scratched the disk a few times and lay down a hip-hop beat. Two bobbed his head along and held the mic up to his face.

*"The Wompalog duck don't fly south for* wint-*a!*
*You don't know what's up, lemme give you a* hint-*a!*
*Double billed, double skilled, rhymin' cup is overfilled,*
*Bilious, but still-ius, my quacking is the shrill-ius.*

*The Wompalog duck got no time to dawdle!*
*The fowl step aside when he starts to waddle!*
*Our yellow-bellied champion is always fightin' for us,*
*DJ! You take over, 'cause I ain't got a chorus."*

The kids shouted and screamed as the DJ kept the beat going. Two pumped his arm to the rhythm for a few seconds more and then stepped off the stage, slipping into the crowd with the mascot head hanging in his right hand. Kids started flowing onto the dance floor, amped up from Two's rap, and Fisher saw his chance. Before anyone

20

could reach Two to congratulate him, Fisher made a dash across the gym and yanked Two into a dark hallway.

"What in the world do you think you're *doing*?" Fisher said, furious. Everything had started off so well.

"I'm roasting in this thing," Two said, throwing the head on the floor and then stripping off the rest of the costume. "And I want to actually *dance* with Amanda, not hover next to her in a plastic cocoon. I took my turn in the suit. Now you can take yours." And he strode back out into the gym before Fisher could stop him.

Fisher kept himself from bolting after Two. No one could see them together; Two wasn't even supposed to exist. Gritting his teeth, he pulled the duck suit on as quickly as he could, trying to ignore the fact that the interior was damp with sweat and smelled like an old gym sock. He popped the head on last of all—it was heavier than he expected—and went off in search of his clone.

From a distance, Fisher watched Two breeze straight past Veronica without saying a word to her. She called after him, confused, but Two kept right on walking like she wasn't there. Fisher balled up his fists and wished desperately that he could rip the suit off and explain everything to Veronica right there.

But there were too many variables. He had no way of knowing how Veronica would react to the news if it was delivered so suddenly. He could do nothing but stew and watch as Two grabbed Amanda and led her in a wild swing dance when the DJ completely changed gears and put a vintage Duke Ellington tune on the turntable.

And Two wasn't even wearing automatic shoes to do it.

Fisher hurried back behind the bleachers and smacked the padded gloves against the walls over and over again, furious and powerless, until he was finally struck with a simple idea. He took out his phone. He sent the quickest and simplest text he could think of to Veronica: Sorry. Will explain. Meet outside in 5?

He let out a long breath, nearly collapsing against the bleachers. Then Two walked up to the punch and poured himself a glass. And Veronica walked up behind him. Fisher was just close enough to hear their conversation.

"Fisher?" Veronica said. "You mind telling me what's going on?"

"What do you mean?" Two said, not even turning his head, and instead shoving a bunch of chips in his mouth.

"I mean." Veronica took a deep breath. "I thought you and I were kind of here . . . like, together."

Two shrugged. "You got the wrong guy," he said.

Veronica looked as if she'd just been slapped in the face with a giant wet noodle. Without saying another word, she spun around and stalked out of the gym. Fisher knew she wasn't going to wait for him outside. She probably wouldn't even look at her phone until she was already back home and cursing the day she'd ever met him.

His hands were shaking inside the fuzzy wings of his costume. Two had caused trouble before, but this time he'd gone too far. And he was going to answer for it.

# ⟫ CHAPTER 3 ⟪

*Ah, yes . . . the school dance. I remember mine fondly. Mostly because I coated the floor with a friction-activated gel that turns shoe leather into a stew-like liquid.*

*—Dr. X, backstage on Family Feudalism*

Two was taking a break in between songs when Fisher struck. He grabbed on to his clone's arm with the grip of a starving cobra and hauled him out into the hallway and to the cafeteria kitchen, where the extra refreshments for the dance were being stored. Fisher whipped off his mask and began stripping off the stupid mascot costume. Dim fluorescent light spilled across carts full of cookies, ridged potato chips, and scarlet punch.

Fisher and Two, identical, and identically angry, squared off.

"We had an agreement," Fisher said, his teeth clamped together. "You got to spend two weeks being a celebrity, living in an LA apartment for free and going to parties and fancy dinners every night. The very *least* you owe me is a single night at a school dance with the girl of my dreams."

"Are you forgetting why I went to LA in the first place?" Two said, crossing his arms. "It was your fault. I was chasing down a lie *you* told me."

They slowly began circling each other, framed by the snacks and drinks.

"Is that why you did this?" Fisher said. "Revenge? You're still angry with me because I kept you in the dark, so you're ruining the one successful interaction I have ever had with another human being?!" He could feel his cheeks and neck starting to flush. Anger poured through his veins like a bubbling beaker of hydrochloric acid. He balled up his fists.

"You would have ruined it with Veronica, anyway," Two said, his voice rising in pitch. "You've never known how to deal with people. If you knew how to deal with people, you wouldn't be so frantic to keep me a secret. If you knew how to deal with people, you'd have told me the truth from the beginning. If you knew how to deal with people, you could've handled the seventh grade, and you never would've made me in the first place!" His voice had risen to a barking shout.

"So that's it?" Fisher shouted back. "You wish you'd never been born??"

"Why not??" Two roared. "You've always treated me like a mistake, anyway!"

*"Well, maybe I should correct it, then!!"* Fisher hurled

at the top of his lungs, before leaping at Two with his arms outstretched.

They locked arms in the middle of the room, pushing against each other with all of their limited might. Fisher had no idea how to fight, and though Two was better at improvising, he really had no idea, either. So they shoved and shouted and grunted at each other.

Two finally freed himself of Fisher's grasp and wound up for a punch. Fisher saw it coming and ducked under Two's fist, bellowing in fury and throwing his shoulder into Two's stomach. Two fell backward, crashing against a cart carrying a bowl of punch and upending the bowl all over his head.

Fisher, who had also fallen, got to his feet, every breath feeling like a match being lit in his throat. Two pulled himself off the floor. The punch had stained his white dress shirt pink. There was also a bright red stain covering the middle of his face, which looked like some large birthmark.

His hair had gone directly into the punch, and was now a dark, reddish shade. Two was about to charge at Fisher again when he caught a glimpse of himself in one of the polished cafeteria doors.

"There," he said, panting. "Are you happy? We're not twins anymore. I'm going back out to the dance. Say hello to your cousin Jimmy." And he gave a short bow and stalked back toward the dance.

Fisher finally felt like he could breathe again. "I don't think so," he panted out. "We're not done yet!"

Two broke into a run as Fisher came after him. Fisher caught the clone just as they reached the gym, and tackled him to the floor. They rolled back and forth, and Two managed to get in two punches. Fisher rolled out of the way, more shocked than hurt, and felt something jab him in the thigh. There was a clicking sound.

Then he remembered: the pocket fireworks display.

Fisher managed to shove Two away from him as a crackling, like demonic popcorn, drowned out the pumping dance music. Moments later, his pocket was blown right off his tux pants with a rush of flame and eight-colored smoke.

Fisher was lucky he'd made the lining of his tux pants flame retardant for exactly this situation. The fireworks spiraled around the gym, leaving bright smoke trails in their wake. The dance chaperones were suddenly on their feet. Shouting filled the room. Fortunately, he had designed the fireworks to burn themselves out quickly, and they dissolved harmlessly in the air after a few seconds, letting off showers of colored sparks.

But people continued shouting. Fisher heard several people scream his name in unison.

He hauled himself up from the floor, arms shaking, his pants ruined. Two was doubled over, panting.

Fisher's heart dropped.

There was a trail of crushed cookies and shattered snack foods leading away from the buffet tables, which had been overturned. The trail led up to the DJ's stage.

It was the duck. Or rather—it was someone *inside* the duck suit.

Disguised, the person was setting out to destroy the gym. The DJ stood up as the unidentified aggressor pushed over one of the four huge speakers around the stage. Kids jumped out of the way as it crashed down, letting off sparks and smoke.

"Fisher?!" someone shouted. "What are you doing?"

Fisher and Two looked at each other, gaping. Then Fisher understood. Everyone had seen Two take off the mask on stage earlier. They all thought it was Fisher in the suit.

Amanda fought her way through the panicked crowd to them.

"Fisher?" she said, confused. "That's not you?"

"Not me," he said, putting up his hands.

"And it's not you . . . ," she said, looking at Two with confusion. "Why are you both here? What happened to you?" She pointed to his cherry-infused face.

"Tell you later," Two said. "First, let's . . ."

But he didn't get to finish his sentence. The duck-suited attacker had grabbed the DJ and chucked him off the stage, where he was fortunately caught by the crowd. The duck slid behind the DJ's computer and began playing wild, thumping beats at such volume that people began falling to the floor, gripping their ears.

Fisher felt like his skull was being excavated with TNT. He collapsed to the floor with Amanda and Two. Trembling, he was able to reach into his inside pockets, withdrawing a small box containing one of his dance-related inventions. He had invented a breath mint so dense that it would take hours to dissolve. He could keep one in his mouth for the whole dance and never worry that his breath's freshness was in peril.

He was counting on that density to save his tortured ears as he popped a mint into each. The sound was still deafening, but no longer crippling. There were two mints left, and after giving Two a scorching look, he handed them over. Two tapped Amanda with worried eyes, and she nodded back that she was okay.

"Just get him!" she screamed. Her voice was barely audible over the crushing remix.

Fisher and Two took off toward the stage, stepping and hopping over their fellow students, who were writhing on the floor in agony. The chaperones were all slumped over in their seats or pressed flat to the floor, moaning, as though hoping the sound waves might simply pass over them.

The mascot leapt from the stage and took off, ducking

around the overturned buffet table and using it as a shield, then sprinting toward the double doors and into the hall. Fisher and Two pursued him all the way out of Wompalog's front doors.

Whoever was inside the duck suit, he was *fast*. Fisher's heart was pounding like the music still echoing from the gym. Two finally caught up to the mascot and leapt onto his back. With amazing strength, the disguised villain kept running. But Two slowed him down, and Fisher managed to catch them. Working together, they tackled the mascot and pinned him to the ground.

Two pried the mask off. There was nothing underneath it.

Still, it kept fighting.

"Someone's rigged it!" Fisher said. "You can see the wires inside!"

"Hold it still!" Two said. "I'll pull the power coupling."

Fisher gripped the suit as tightly as he could as Two reached down into its neck, grabbing wires where he could. The mascot gave three more weak thrashes before falling still.

Fisher collapsed in a heap as Two stood up.

"Was this your plan for me?" Two said. "Put me in this suit and try to control it with wires and controls?"

"Don't be ridiculous," Fisher said. "I didn't know anything about this."

"Sure," Two said. "And I bet you—"

*"Fisher Bas!"* thundered a deep voice, cutting Two off.

Principal Teed strode across Wompalog's front lawn, where Fisher still lay in a heap with the mascot suit. His face was as bright red as the punch in Two's hair. "I thought I'd seen your worst when you stormed the cafeteria with King of Hollywood French fries last month," he said in a growl, "but you've well and truly made a wreck of things this time. Your capacity for destruction and mayhem amazes me! The formal is one of the most anticipated events of the year, and you've ruined it for everyone! Do you realize the damage you've caused? Do you think all of this is funny? *Well?!*"

He looked back and forth between Fisher, who had sprung to his feet, and Two.

"Are you a relative of his, young man?" he finally asked Two, frowning.

"Cousin, sir," Two said with feigned meekness and without skipping a beat. "I chased him out here to try and talk some sense into him." Fisher shot a poison dart look at Two, but the clone kept his eyes on Mr. Teed.

"Huh. Good luck with that," the principal scoffed, before turning back to Fisher. "What you did was absolutely inexcusable. A prank is one thing, but that kind of disruption . . ." He paused to suck in a deep breath. The red in his face started to fade.

"Listen, Fisher," he said, in a slightly calmer voice. "We all remember the TechX explosion. I realize that you went through a horrible experience that you're still recovering from. Ordinarily, I'd expel a student instantly for pulling a prank like this. But I have to take your recent trauma into account. For now, go home. I'll think about what to do with you later."

Fisher stood up. He found he had nothing to say. Behind Mr. Teed, the students poured out on the lawn, and they whispered and pointed at him. He saw the Vikings, looking gleeful. He saw Veronica, looking disgusted.

He realized he was on the verge of tears.

So he simply turned around and started for home.

His automated dance shoes slapped the sidewalk dully as he passed under the glow of the street lamps. It seemed like he kept climbing to higher and higher peaks, only to find a sheer cliff on the other side and plummet down again. The relationship he'd been building with Veronica was shattered, his friendship with Two had ended in a fight, and his hero status at the school had officially been revoked.

But it was more than that. The way the mascot suit had come alive, had sliced a destructive path through the dance . . .

Only two people Fisher knew had both the ability and the evil nature to rig such a feat. And one of them was far away, filming an awful reality TV show.

Fisher was still turning the night's events over and over in his mind an hour later as he lay on his bed, avoiding his parents, staring at the ceiling, petting FP, and hating his life.

He heard the remote-activated ladder attached to his window turn on. A minute later, Two climbed in through the window.

"I didn't think you'd have the guts to come back here," Fisher said coldly as Two pressed a button to retract the ladder. He started to roll over to face the wall and caught a glimpse of Two's face. He was white as a sheet. "What is it?" Fisher asked.

"I . . . searched the mascot after you left," Two said. He no longer sounded angry. He sounded afraid. He held out a piece of paper. "I found this."

Fisher took it. It was a postcard with a picture of the Hollywood sign. On the back, in small, exceptionally neat print much like their own, was written a simple message: *That was only the beginning. There will be more. Much more.*

Fisher felt like his blood had been replaced with arctic wind.

"Three's here."

That was only
the beginning.
There will be more.
Much more.

# ≋ CHAPTER 4 ≋

Talking about what you've done is different when what you've done can talk about you.

—Fisher Bas, Extended Clone Log

Fisher stood in the living room, hands clasped behind his back. His parents were seated in front of him, concern on their faces. Fisher breathed as slowly and as deeply as he could. A hasty breath might send his diaphragm and larynx into uncontrollable spasms.

His parents had been informed about the "incident" at the dance the night before. Baffled by the change in Fisher's behavior, they, like Principal Teed, had hypothesized that Fisher's experience at TechX might be having a lasting posttraumatic effect on him.

But Fisher knew he'd been dragging the illusion on for far too long. His lie about Two was sucking dry so much of his energy, which could be of use elsewhere. If they were going to stop Three, they would have to give 100 percent effort. Nothing less would ever succeed, not against an enemy so clever and so cold.

The time had come to stop the charade, and he finally had his parents' attention from their current top-secret project.

"I hope you asked us down here because you have a good explanation for what happened at the dance," his mother said. She was in her usual lab attire, which included a pair of sophisticated goggles hanging around her neck and large, acid-proof gloves. "I have compounds synthesizing upstairs. I can't leave them unattended for long."

"I've got a colony of ants in the early stage of collective consciousness," said his father. "Also, my cyborg antelope used its electro-antlers to short out one of my best microscopes, and I need to fix it." A tiny pair of dark scorch spots on his left pant leg suggested that the antelope hadn't stopped at the microscope.

"I know you're both busy," Fisher said, "and that I've been acting a little . . . strange lately. But this is important. Very, very important. Probably the most important thing I've ever told you."

Mr. and Mrs. Bas looked at each other, then back at Fisher, clearly worried about what might come next. Mr. Bas's spring-supported spectroscopic eyepiece hung from its headband perch, and he reached up and brushed it out of the way.

"I . . . have someone I'd like you to meet," Fisher said, suppressing the very strong urge to back away until he was within leaping distance of the nearest window. "Come on out," he said in a louder voice, stepping slightly to the side.

Two walked into the room, the remnants of the punch stain on his face not quite scrubbed out, and stood next to Fisher.

There was a long period of complete, suffocating silence. Fisher's mind went to a recent Vic Daring storyline in which the space scoundrel was placed on trial for theft of an imperial Martian ruby, and stood before the planet's rulers in an immense court chamber carved from stone, and was flanked by various Martian gladiatorial beasts. He really hoped his dad hadn't engineered any of those lately.

"Hi," said Two at last.

Fisher's parents looked back and forth between the two boys.

"The missing Accelerated Growth Hormone," his mother said. "The compound that got stolen from my lab . . . did . . . is this Dr. X's work?" Fisher could tell from her expression that even as she said it, she knew it wasn't.

"No," he said, lowering his head. "It's mine. My work, my responsibility."

Silence fell over the room like a five-ton boulder. Fisher's parents stared at the fidgeting Two for a long time, then looked at each other, astounded.

"That's . . . that's . . . ," his mother said, grasping for words. She was obviously torn between anger at Fisher for taking the AGH and making Two, and marvel that he had accomplished such a staggering feat of biological engineering.

"Why did you do it, Fisher?" his dad said, since his mom was still speechless.

"I . . . couldn't take things at Wompalog," Fisher said. "Ignored, beat up, trampled, harassed. I thought I saw a way out and I took it. I didn't think about the consequences. I'm sorry."

"The Fisher you knew the week before the TechX explosion was really me," Two said. "I was the one making trouble at school, and I was the one who got kidnapped. Fisher risked his life springing me out of Dr. X's compound, and together we destroyed the place."

They had agreed to keep the Los Angeles adventure and the threat of Three to themselves for now. They knew that their parents would try to prevent them from fighting Three, to keep them out of harm's way. But Fisher and Two were the best suited to take on the new clone. Like it or not, he was made of mostly the same stuff that they were.

Mostly.

Because when Dr. X had made Three, he had used Fisher's DNA as a basis, but bent it. Warped it, shaped it, and twisted it until it resembled something very different. Three looked like them, but he was stronger and tougher. More importantly, he was nearly emotionless.

Cruel. Cold as a dagger blade and just as dangerous.

Fisher's mother stood up, stepped forward, and regarded Two more closely. Then she turned back to Fisher.

"I can understand what you did, however foolish it was. But it's not the fact that you stole from me that bothers me most. It's the fact that you lied to us. All this time, you lied to us."

"I know," Fisher said, feeling his whole body tensing up in a giant cringe. "I've felt more awful about that than I ever imagined I could feel."

"I can see that," she replied. "I realize now I saw the signs of it all along. Oh, Fisher," she said, shaking her head with a little smile. "Nothing I could do to punish you could make you feel worse than you must have already felt."

Fisher peeked at her to make sure she wasn't kidding. He realized, suddenly, that his parents weren't angry. Their faces weren't swirling vortexes of electricity preparing to blast him into oblivion. And he knew a swirling vortex of electricity when he saw one; he'd seen his dad create one by accident once. It had almost blown the back of the house off.

"You have the intellect for incredible things," his dad said, standing up to join his mother. "I mean, we've got one of the most amazing accomplishments in scientific

39

history standing in front of us. But you need to learn some discipline."

"When kids hear the word *discipline*, they think of punishment," his mom said. "But that's not what *discipline* means. It means being able to control your mind and use your skills wisely. It means taking responsibility for the result of your work. We've given you so many tools, but I don't think we ever really taught you scientific discipline."

"I think I see where you're going with this," his dad said to his mom. "Fisher, you're going to be our home lab assistant for a while. Science, just like any other profession, isn't only about genius equations, new inventions, and brilliant ideas. It's about work. Long, hard, boring work. The end result wouldn't be nearly as special if it wasn't."

"You'll help us keep our labs clean, calibrate our instruments, double-check measurements, compare data," his mother said.

"Care for the genetically engineered bugs that've developed a taste for mushroom and eggplant pizza . . . ," his dad added in with a low sigh.

"You get the idea," his mom finished. "Is that a little less catastrophic than what you'd imagined?"

Fisher waited a few seconds, in case that electrical vortex was just a bit late in charging up. But they really meant it. He nodded, and cold relief flooded him so fast, he almost lost his footing. Telling Two the truth had felt sort of like this, and it was nice to welcome that feeling back.

"And as for you," his mom said, turning to look at Two, who'd been standing quietly, for once in his short life, "we'd always thought about what it would be like to have another child. We didn't imagine it would happen on such short notice, but welcome to the Bas family, er . . . What is your name, anyway?"

"Two," said Two.

"I think we can do better than an integer," his dad said. "We named Fisher after your mom's father. I think it's only fair that my dad gets a chance." He smiled.

"Welcome home, Alexander," said his mom, hugging the clone formerly known as Two, who, after a moment of shock, hugged her right back.

"As in, the Great?" he said. "I like it! *Alex* for short?"

"Of course," said his dad.

"Though for that little stunt in the cafeteria, young man, you'll be playing lab assistant for a while, too," Mrs. Bas said, looking at him with only a half-stern expression.

And there they were. Fisher and Alex Bas, no longer boy and clone, but real brothers. Not that that would necessarily be a widely known fact, as their parents were quick to point out.

# HOME LAB
# ASSISTANT SCHEDULE
## FOR FISHER AND ALEX

AM BEFORE SCHOOL:
- DUST LAB GLASSWARE AND COUNTERS
- RUN CALIBRATION ON SCALES, THERMOMETERS, BURNERS AND ALL ELECTRONIC MONITORS

PM AFTER SCHOOL:
- DOUBLE-CHECK MEASUREMENTS, COMPARE AND ANALYZE DAY'S DATA
- CLEAN GENETICALLY ENGINEERED BUG CAGES
- WATER AND CONVERSE WITH GENETICALLY ENGINEERED PLANTS
- MOP FLOOR - USE DAD'S HAIR GEL (FORMULATE MORE IF NECESSARY)

They'd keep up the cousin story and get Alex properly enrolled at Wompalog. Their mom promised to get Alex some hair dye that wasn't corn syrup and food coloring. There was a spare room that was being used to store lab equipment, and they got to work clearing it out to make a new bedroom.

Later that afternoon, Fisher sat in his room, scratching FP, who lay in his lap asleep after finding a jar of peanut butter and spending several hours sucking the entire thing out through a thin crack in its plastic side.

It would be weird having his whole room to himself again. As frustrating as Two . . . Alex, he had to keep correcting himself, could get, the company had been welcome.

But he was happy. Happier than he'd been, probably, since inventing Two (Alex!) in the first place. He felt as if badgers had been gnawing his stomach for the past few weeks. Now they were gone. The truth was finally out.

But there was no time to rest now. Now the work would really begin. Three was here, and he was capable of anything.

And only the Bas boys could stop him.

# ≋ CHAPTER 5 ≋

At first, I thought the people here acted the way they do because it was an evil villain's academy. But no villain could ever be evil and brilliant enough to create something as fiendish as the seventh grade.

—Alex Bas, Journal

*Whoosh.*

Alex's hand sailed through empty air as Sebastian Wong withdrew his hand at the last moment and instead smoothed his hair back.

"I don't think so," Sebastian said. He and his friends started laughing. It was the third high five Alex had been denied in two minutes.

Alex looked down at his hand like it was a flashlight that had run out of batteries.

"Fisher . . . nobody's talking to me," he said as they walked down the halls of Wompalog between third and fourth periods on Monday morning.

"Get back to me about that after you've experienced it for twelve more years," Fisher said.

Fisher's parents had managed to put together a speedy offense to get their surprise new son enrolled at the school, who was still posing as Fisher's cousin from Massachusetts. Ever since Fisher had revealed the truth about Alex to their parents, the brothers had been getting along again. Which was good, because it seemed nobody else would give them the time of day—not even the short-est, flimsiest second.

Alex wasn't the new, cool incarnation of Fisher any-more. And Fisher wasn't the bold spy hero who'd destroyed TechX and saved the town. Now they were the two horse-men of the fall formal apocalypse. Everyone believed that they were responsible for everything the destructive mas-cot had done, and the other kids avoided them like they had a flesh-eating disease transmitted by eye contact.

Fisher hadn't even seen Veronica. He'd gotten an e-mail from her over the weekend accusing him of secretly being after Amanda.

*I knew she was your friend,* she'd written. *And I'd have been happy to let you have a dance with her if you'd just asked me. But you snuck away, disguised yourself, and ignored me when I came to find you. The fact that you tried to hide it from me tells me all I need to know. When I asked you to the formal, you could've just said no. And now I wish you had.*

The message—the last sentence especially—floated in front of Fisher's eyes in big, ugly neon pink letters. Not literally, although he had been working on a holographic text display device—but far worse: in his mind, where he had no power to resize, delete, replace, or minimize it.

Now that Two was Alex and known to the world, Fisher hoped that he could explain and fix everything with her. But first she'd have to actually give him the chance to do it.

He'd also have to come up with some kind of story explaining the mascot incident. Maybe he could say it'd been Alex in the suit the whole time; he'd just been joking around and it'd gotten out of hand. Maybe he could say that he'd detected a dangerous power surge in the DJ's equipment and had thrown the DJ off the stage for his own protection, and taken over the console to try and stop it.

It was disturbing to Fisher how quickly the lies began forming in his head. That was the problem with lying: it was a difficult habit to break.

"This is really how it was?" said Alex, after waving at a passing classmate who pretended to notice something extremely important on the toe of his own shoe.

"All day, every day," said Fisher. "I haven't seen the Vikings yet, but now that nobody's looking, they'll swoop in the first chance they get. Is everything in place? You didn't forget the key ingredient?"

"In place," Alex said. "If they attack, we'll be ready for them."

"I hope so," Fisher said. "Well, this is me," he said, stopping outside a classroom. "See you later, *cousin.*"

"Yeah . . . later."

Fisher walked into English. As he'd expected, the other kids immediately averted their eyes and shrank away like he was trailing a cloud of frost. Sighing, he settled into a seat in the back row and removed a sheet of paper from his backpack. It was a map of Palo Alto, marked with a grid.

Careful analysis of the circuitry that Three had installed in the DBYBBD duck suit had yielded some samples of dust and dirt, which Fisher and Alex had carefully collected for analysis. When Mr. Bas had been looking for the best habitat in Palo Alto for the *real* double-billed yellow-bellied bilious duck, he had gotten dirt samples from locations all over the city. As soon as Fisher could compare the chemical makeup of the residue in the suit to his dad's samples, he could find out where the duck suit had been rewired—and find Three.

His calculations assumed, of course, that Three was staying in one place. Maybe he was moving around. Or maybe he wasn't even here. Maybe he was working from an island off the coast, in a stone fortress shaped like a skull.

He really didn't know much about Three, but he knew enough not to rule anything out.

# Calculations of
# ESTIMATED ODDS OF
# HIDING PLACES FOR THREE

N
↑

PALO ALTO, CA

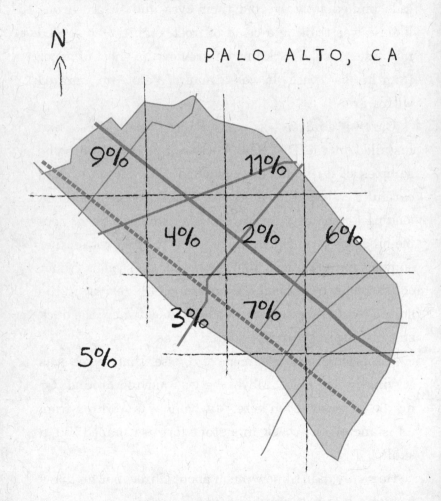

9%

11%

4%   2%   6%

3%   7%

5%

Fisher thought about Three's flat, freezing eyes, and how close he and Two had come to disintegration at his hands. Why couldn't the new clone have just quietly vanished? Made up a new name and glued on a big fake mustache and lived a nice, quiet life in the middle of South Dakota or something?

The night before, Fisher and Two had decided to e-mail their friend Agent Mason for help. The man Fisher had originally met as a sound tech named Henry had turned out to be with the FBI. He'd let Fisher and Two go after securing Dr. X's AGH sample. Fisher knew they could trust him. But so far, Mason hadn't written back.

In the meanwhile, Fisher and Two took another shot at modifying the DNA-based detector Fisher had originally developed to help him find Two in LA. But once again, the trial failed when they'd set the detector on the floor between them and it had spun like a propeller, pointing back and forth between them furiously, before beginning to smoke.

Class crawled by at the speed of an inchworm crossing the Sahara. Fisher's attention drifted in and out, and the next two classes dragged on at a similar pace.

It was just before lunch when he spotted Veronica and hurried to catch up with her.

"Fisher," she said tonelessly by way of a greeting.

"Veronica," Fisher said. His pulse gunned to life after

flowing like slush in a drainpipe all day. "Listen, I have to—"

"Save it," she said. "I don't want to hear it. I . . . I don't know what to think of you anymore. I'm very disappointed and a little shocked. And I'd rather not talk to you for a while. At all. That's it, I guess. Bye, Fisher."

Fisher tried to say something, but all that came out was an anguished grunt. He felt like she had one end of his soul in her hand and it was slowly unspooling as she walked away, growing smaller and fainter. It was the only conversation he'd had today with someone other than his clone. Being ignored was starting to feel friendly by comparison.

The cafeteria buzz seemed to get quieter in a little bubble around Fisher. He got his food as quickly as he could and found the otherwise empty table where Alex was sitting.

"How's it going?" Alex asked, as if he didn't know.

"Not fast enough," Fisher said.

"At least we have our . . . meat loaf? . . . to console us?" Alex answered, staring down quizzically at his lunch.

"I thought it was banana bread," Fisher said, poking at the substance. "Hm. Maybe I'll just stick with the baked potato. It's pretty hard to mess those up. We all set here?"

"The materials are in place," Alex said, tapping something beneath the table with his foot. "Now we just have to wait. How's the baked potato?"

"I could use a pickax," said Fisher.

"Mine may require dynamite," said Alex.

As Fisher leaned over Alex's lunch tray, his neck hairs began to stand up. He instantly recognized the familiar feeling of being loomed over.

He looked up . . . and up . . . and up, and saw three broad, flat faces staring grimly down at them, like a Mount Rushmore of Cro-Magnons. As always, Brody in the middle, Leroy and Willard on either side. The Vikings.

"Too bad about the formal," said Brody.

"Too b-bad," said Willard.

"You spoiled a big vocation," said Leroy.

"Occasion," said Brody, expression unchanging. There was nothing that could be done to salvage Leroy's vocabulary. "And oh, look, there's two Bases now." He smiled a mouthful of gray, chipped teeth. Years of open-faced candy corn sandwiches on French toast had seen to that. "How fun."

"So?" Fisher said. "What are you gonna do about it?"

Brody's smile dropped faster than his grades. "You still think you're a big shot, huh?" he said, leaning over the table. When Fisher and Alex failed to run away in terror, he frowned. "We're gonna teach you a lesson! Now get up."

"No," Fisher said, taking a sip of his water. He was impressed that his hands were steady.

"What'd you just say?" Brody said, looming as large as he could.

"I'm sorry, that may have gone over your head," said Alex, picking at his potato. "We're researching a simpler word for *no*, but linguistics isn't really our specialty. Please be patient."

"Why you little . . . ," Brody said. "Flip the table!" he shouted to his fellow thugs.

The three Vikings took the edge of the table and heaved. The table didn't move.

"Forgot to mention," Fisher said, "we've been testing a fast-acting, extremely powerful adhesive. We used it to glue the table to the floor."

Brody growled and tried to pull his arm back for a punch. But couldn't.

"Oh, also," said Alex, "we applied a liberal amount to the edge you just grabbed."

The Vikings planted their feet and pulled as hard as they could, but even their tree stump–like physiques proved incapable of breaking the glue's bond. All six of their hands were stuck fast.

"Unstick us, you d-despicable stick figures!" said Willard, thrashing from side to side.

"You know, there is one thing that can dissolve the glue," Alex said, standing up and walking in a little circle around the trapped bullies.

"What?? What??" said Brody.

"Honey barbecue sauce," said Fisher, getting up from his seat. "Remind me of the proportions you need, cousin?"

"You need a one-thousand-to-one-sauce-to-glue ratio," Alex responded. "But I think we can make that work."

Fisher and Alex hauled a drink cooler the size of a small chair out from under the table. Fisher popped off the top. Other kids had noticed what was going on, and the chatter got louder around them.

"Okay," he said. "We can help you. But you have to ask nicely."

"Fisher," said Brody. "I'll wring your tiny, little—"

"Oh man," Alex said. "Did that sound nice to you, Fisher?"

"It didn't even sound like asking, Alex," Fisher said. By now the students nearby were pointing and giggling. Fisher and Alex started to walk away.

"Wait! Wait!" Brody said. "You gotta let us go!"

"You ever hear of the magic word, fellas?" said Alex. Brody gritted his teeth so hard, his back shook.

*"Please,"* he mumbled under his breath.

"Please do what, exactly?" Fisher said, tapping the cooler.

*"Pleasepourbarbecuesauceonus,"* he said, as fast as he could.

"Didn't quite catch that," Alex said, cupping one hand to his ear.

*"Please pour barbecue sauce on us!!"* Brody screamed in rage.

Everyone in the cafeteria was looking. Fisher and Alex hefted the heavy container and unleashed upon each Viking a gallon or so of the viscous, sweet-smelling condiment. There was a moment of shocked silence, and then a roar of cheers and laughter.

Fisher and Alex stood back as the Vikings' hands slowly came unstuck. As soon as they were loose, the three towering statues of honey-barbecue goodness charged at the brothers. But Alex pulled something that looked like a normal ballpoint pen from his pocket and held it in the air, shaking his head in warning.

The Vikings stopped in their tracks, turned on their heels, and bolted.

"What is that?" Fisher said.

"Ballpoint pen," said Alex. "But they don't know that." He grinned.

The laughing and cheering continued.

"Looks like we may have won back a few hearts," Alex said, motioning around the cafeteria, where people were clapping and smiling. Even Gassy Greg let off an enormous, approving fart. Fisher noticed, however, that Veronica was still seated, arms tightly crossed, scowling.

"And earned a detention," Fisher said as two teachers charged toward them. "Let's make our exit while we can."

They slipped out of the cafeteria and into a side alcove lined with lockers. They saw both teachers speed past them, heading in a totally different direction. Fisher sighed and leaned back against the lockers. He was glad they'd stood up to the Vikings. But getting into trouble was tiring.

"Good going."

He looked up and saw Amanda. Her black hair was cut like a curtain across her forehead, and the tank top she was wearing showed off arms toned from the wrestling club.

"Amanda!" Alex cried out. Then he quickly tried to regain his composure, sweeping a hand through his hair. "I mean, um, hi. I mean, thank you."

Amanda crossed her arms. "Either of you want to tell me what happened at the formal?"

"It's Three," Fisher said.

"That was his way of saying hello," Alex said.

"Wow," Amanda said. "I wonder how he says, 'I don't like you.'"

"So do we," said Alex, giving Fisher a grave look. "So do we."

# CHAPTER 6

*I destroyed the robot fortress like you asked. There was nothing in the contract about how you wanted the planet the fortress was located on to end up.*

*—Vic Daring, Issue #452*

Fisher stood in the lobby of the movie theatre at the Westbury Mall, wringing his hands together.

After school the day before, Alex had at last convinced Fisher to take a break from obsessing over Three's whereabouts and deal with his other major problem: Veronica. He'd called her, and she'd agreed to listen to what he had to say—although for twenty minutes, she had not spoken a single word, and he was only sure that she hadn't hung up because he could hear the sounds of her breathing.

He'd explained that his cousin Alex had been rude to her at the dance and had danced with Amanda Cantrell. He just prayed she'd believe it; Alex's hair had not yet been dyed then. Then again, the gym had been dark. Finally, he'd heard a little sniff, which he took as a sign of encouragement.

So he'd plunged on. He told her the mascot had acted on its own, that afterward he'd discovered an automated system built into it, and that it had looked like something leftover from the Dr. X days. All of that was true. He wasn't quite ready to tell anyone else about Three yet. Not before he knew where Three was hiding.

By then she was speaking in full sentences, and Fisher's heart was floating somewhere in space.

Then he'd nervously, haltingly asked her to the movies after school the next day. She'd agreed.

So here he was. He'd arrived well in advance of their meeting time partly out of sheer nerves and partly because he'd been forced to bring FP along with him. His parents were out of the house and he didn't trust the little pink tornado to be left alone.

Since as far as he knew, pigs were not allowed in the theatre, Fisher had rigged a disguise for him. FP was wearing a specially fitted garment that looked like an ordinary pet sweater. But a quick string pull reversed and expanded it, making FP look like a packaged loaf of pumpernickel bread. It was very realistic, especially in the tote bag Fisher was using to carry him.

There was also a compartment above FP's head that could hold a cubic foot of snack foods for the always-hungry pig to eat. Fisher periodically snuck a handful of popcorn into it from the barrel-sized container he'd bought.

Fisher paced the lobby, sneaking FP food, and absentmindedly watching the TV mounted in the corner, behind the refreshments stand. Then a report came on that caught his attention. It was about *Family Feudalism*, the Granger brothers' show.

"Ratings for this fifteenth-century-themed reality program are topping the charts," said the reporter, "but is it causing family members to truly 'go medieval' on one another? Reports show a dramatic increase in arguments and altercations within families that directly corresponds to *Family Feudalism* viewership. More after this."

The report changed to something else and Fisher lost interest. It was probably just another one of those "scandals," like how your morning coffee is slowly melting your rib cage. He had *real* problems to worry about.

His calculations hadn't gotten him any closer to locating Three. And there'd been no word back from Special Agent Mason. Alex and Fisher had discussed it with Amanda, who had proven to be a valuable ally. She'd responded cryptically that she might know someone who could help. Fisher prayed that was true.

Finally, the door opened and Veronica walked in. She wasn't exactly smiling, but she wasn't frowning, either. There was a hope in her eyes that gave Fisher some hope of his own.

"Hi," she said, alternating her gaze between Fisher and the floor.

"I'm glad you're here," Fisher said, and reached for his

back pocket. "I've got something for you. Been working on it for weeks."

"Really?" she said.

Fisher pulled a capsule about the size of an aspirin from his back pocket. The Rose Pill was a painstakingly researched project, involving complex genetic, biological, physiological, chemical, and engineering work. This would be its first field test. Veronica stared down at the tiny capsule, confused.

Fisher rubbed the pill between his palms, and then opened his hands again. The Rose Pill was activated by heat and friction.

It was just as he had planned.

What he hadn't planned was how long the stems grew, and the fact that roots were emerging from their undersides. Fisher and Veronica jumped back as a rosebush the size of a maple tree sprouted up, its roots digging into the lobby's carpet. It bloomed into dozens of roses and brushed the big room's ceiling. Everyone stopped what they were doing to stare.

"Excuse me, excuse me," a security guard said, making his way over to Fisher. "I'm afraid we don't allow outside, uh, trees. . . ." His speech trailed off into quiet mumbles. Veronica stifled a giggle.

"I'll tell you what," Fisher said. "You can keep it and use it to decorate your lobby if I can just trim a few roses."

"Uh," the guard said, looking up at the huge plant. "Let me talk to the manager. I'll just . . ." He walked away, still dazed, without finishing the sentence. Fisher pulled a multi-tool from his pocket and used the scissors part to clip four roses, which he handed to an amazed Veronica.

"One thing's for sure, Fisher," she said as she lifted a blossom to her nose, "you are a source of constant surprises."

Two hours later, they walked out of *I Can Tell a Lie*, an alternate-history movie in which George Washington was really an Italian con man and the whole American Revolution was a masterful scam he plotted with the British to weaken the colonies. It was entertaining, if a bit of a stretch plot wise.

FP was asleep in his bread disguise, having gone through all the snacks Fisher could throw at him and passing out twenty minutes into the movie. Veronica was finally smiling. Back in the lobby, maintenance workers were putting a little fence and some benches around their newest decoration.

"Looks like your gardening project is a big hit," Veronica said. "I'm hungry. Want to get a bite?"

"Watching this guy deplete the world's popcorn reserves has given me an appetite," Fisher said, nudging FP through the tote bag. "What do you feel like?"

"I feel indecisive," Veronica said, scratching her cheek.

"Food court?"

"Works for me," said Fisher.

Voices ricocheted off the linoleum, amplified by the high ceilings. The Westbury Mall was large and full of light. Fountains sprayed colored water from steel-mounted jets. Fisher wasn't much of a shopper, but while walking next to Veronica in the mall, he thought the Westbury might be his new favorite place.

Still, he couldn't quite relax. It was so crowded. So many people . . . and Three could be anywhere. Fisher found himself checking to his left and right, and glancing over his shoulder with almost every step. He felt a lot like he had in LA, when government agents were on his tail. He'd only gotten out of that mess thanks to Agent Mason's quick thinking.

As they got off the escalator on the mall's second floor, they saw Alex walking in their direction, next to what appeared to be a massive plastic tub with legs.

"Oh, hey, Fisher! Hi, Veronica." Alex said, coming up to them. His companion, it turned out, was not a walking plastic tub, but Amanda, who set down the heavy drum of protein powder she'd been carrying.

"Oh . . . Hi," Veronica said, with a thin, brittle smile in Alex's direction. The cousin-clone's existence was something she was still getting used to, and the way he'd acted toward her in the dance probably still stung.

"Hey," Fisher said. He nodded at Amanda. "You planning to eat that or bathe in it?"

"I have a wrestling match coming up," she said. "Got to be sure I'm at peak strength."

"We were just about to get a bite to eat," Alex said. "You want to join us?"

"That's okay," Veronica said.

At the same time, Fisher said, "Sounds great!" Immediately, he felt like an idiot.

"How does the Rainforest Cafe sound to you two?" Alex said.

"All right," Veronica said. She even managed to smile. "That's my favorite restaurant."

"They've got some kind of animal show going on. It seems like *just* what we've been looking for." Alex gave Fisher a subtle head nod. Fisher wasn't sure what Alex meant. He was just happy they were going to Veronica's favorite restaurant.

The inside of the Rainforest Cafe was a big, open atrium decorated with an overhang that looked like a low jungle canopy. Leaves and stems in a dozen shades of green shared space with thick vines and occasional bursts of huge orange, yellow, and red tropical flowers. On one side of the restaurant, a makeshift stage had been erected behind an enormous fake tree. Fisher saw Amanda nudge Alex and gesture to it meaningfully. She must be really excited about the show.

By the time the waiter arrived, Fisher was finally relaxed. Veronica and Alex were talking about their favorite animals, and Veronica was smiling. FP was hidden beneath the table by Fisher's legs, gnawing on the bread Fisher had been handing down from the basket on the table.

Suddenly, the lights shifted, and a tall man wearing a microphone walked up onto the stage.

"Hello, everyone! I hope you're all enjoying yourselves. My name's Tom, and I run the Phenomenal Fauna Farm! We're an exotic animal show, and I'm pleased to let you know that Rainforest Cafe has hired us to entertain you. So sit back, relax, and enjoy the wildlife!"

Amanda, Fisher noticed, tensed up immediately. If she was so excited about the show, why did she suddenly look ready to sprint out of her seat?

A procession of constrictors came first. Handlers dressed in safari gear walked around the stage with pythons, boas, and other huge snakes draped around them in loops and coils. The patrons clapped and cheered as the snakes gave way to a rainbow of fantastically plumed birds.

"This is amazing, isn't it?" Fisher leaned over to whisper to Veronica.

But no sooner than the words had left his mouth, he was aware of a low whine from under the table, and a sudden burst of pig-sniffing sounds. He ducked his head and saw FP sniffing frantically at the air, ears flat against his head, eyes glittering with excitement.

Fisher knew that look, and his stomach sank.

"No, FP!" he said, and tried to pull FP into his lap.

But it was too late. As if the costume were a giant rubber band and FP were a pebble, the pig burst out of his bread disguise and shot away from the table too quickly for Fisher to even try and catch him.

Fisher almost overturned the table as he jumped up, trying to chase the seemingly rocket-powered FP. Veronica shouted as he accidentally overturned a glass of water in her lap. But he didn't even have time to apologize.

FP careened straight for the stage, where a crowd of smaller mammals from a variety of climates—baby sloths, anteaters, badgers, and others—were preening. FP leapt onto the stage and burst right through the middle of the group. Several animals scattered. The handlers began shouting. The manager of the restaurant started cursing.

Fisher jumped on the stage, dodging the other animals, ducking and tripping through a blur of fur and claws. Finally, he spotted FP, who was locked in a playful tussle with a very familiar-looking animal.

"There he is!" cried Amanda. Fisher hadn't realized she'd followed him.

Suddenly, he understood.

*"Wally?"* he said incredulously as Alex and Amanda hopped onstage to join him.

Wally the Wombat looked up at Fisher and blinked before returning to his swatting match with FP.

Fisher couldn't believe it. Wally the Wombat had been featured on Dr. Devilish's TV show and later turned out to be the trained companion of Agent Mason. So that was what Amanda had meant when she said she would help. Amanda was trying to find Mason by tracking down his animal companion. And she'd tracked him to, of all places, a mall in Palo Alto.

Wally was clearly as excited to see FP as FP was to see him. In fact, they were so excited, they seemed hardly to notice that their antics were causing the other animals to flee the stage and career through the restaurant, over-turning tables, landing on plates and in soup bowls, and causing general panic.

"We'll get Wally!" yelled Alex over the increasing com-motion. "You grab FP!"

Fisher dove into the fray, and was tripped by a scam-pering wallaby. He pulled himself up as Alex managed to chase Wally into Amanda's arms. Fisher scooped up the distracted FP, and the kids made a run for it.

"Come on, Veronica!" Fisher called over the noise.

The restaurant was pandemonium. Birds and bats swooped between the decorative plants, lizards and little mammals were hopping from table to table, and a few big cats prowled. The customers were ducking, dodging, run-ning, and screaming. Fisher led his group out, FP cradled tightly in his arms. They found a path among the wreck-age, leapt over an anaconda as big as a fallen tree trunk, and escaped the restaurant.

They kept going full tilt toward the mall's entrance. The animals were swooping and running and jumping all over the mall, and the only safe bet was for them to get out entirely.

The doors were in sight. Maybe, Fisher prayed, he and

Veronica would laugh about this some day. Like in fifty years.

They were dashing past the mall's coin-filled fountain when a parakeet, appearing out of nowhere, dove straight for Fisher's head. He ducked to the side to avoid it and knocked straight into Veronica.

He turned. Time seemed to slow to an agonizing crawl. He watched Veronica stumble. Her foot caught on the lip of the fountain. Her legs came out from underneath her and she sailed sideways, plunging headfirst into the water, sending a miniature wave sloshing over the side of the fountain.

No, Fisher decided. Fifty years were definitely not enough. If they were ever going to laugh about it, he would need at least a century.

Ten minutes later, they were standing around the corner, waiting for the bus that would take them home. Amanda still had hold of Wally, and Fisher clutched FP. Amanda and Alex had backed away to give Veronica and Fisher privacy. But they needn't have. No one spoke.

Veronica was trying to wring her shirt dry, shivering, her hair in front of her face like a soaked curtain. Fisher couldn't see her eyes, and decided he probably wouldn't want to, anyway.

After long, agonized minutes of silence, Veronica

finally managed to squeeze most of the water out of her shirt and most of the coins out of her hair. At last, she turned to Fisher. He had been right. It was better when he couldn't see her eyes.

"Listen to me, Fisher," she said, in a low, controlled voice. "I think you're a good, well-intentioned person. But I am never, ever going on a date with you again."

Then she turned and walked away, with as much dignity as was possible with her shoes squelching with each step.

Fisher opened his mouth to call out to her, but no words came.

"I'm sorry, Fisher," Alex said, cautiously approaching and patting him on the shoulder.

"Yeah" was all Fisher could muster. His heart felt like it had been split in two and pounded into veal scaloppine.

"Look on the bright side," Amanda said, giving Wally a squeeze. "At least we got ahold of this little guy."

"How did you find him, anyway?" Fisher asked, although at the moment, he didn't even care.

"He has a fan website," Amanda said. "Now I'm hoping we can use him to find Mason. Do you think maybe he's already here? Trying to find Three?" In LA, Agent Mason had set Wally up, on purpose, to be kidnapped by Dr. X along with FP. The wombat had sniffed out Dr. X's vial of Accelerated Growth Hormone, or AGH, and returned it to Mason.

"Maybe," Fisher said. But he didn't even care. All he could think about was Veronica's plunge into freezing fountain water. And the far colder words she'd spoken to him afterward.

The bus was rumbling up to the nearby stop.

"Let's get out of here," Alex said quietly, patting Fisher's shoulder.

Fisher nodded numbly. And with that, they began the long and miserable trip home.

# ≋ CHAPTER 7 ≋

I appreciate the many qualities Dr. X gave me.
I appreciate even more that he kept his humanity to
himself.

—Three, Personal Log

"Ms. Snapper?" said Trevor Weiss, his skinny arm sway-
ing in the air like a riverbank reed in a mild breeze.

Fisher and Alex shot each other a curious look.

First-period biology was no more than a post-breakfast
nap for most of their classmates. Ms. Snapper had gotten
used to the slumped bodies, the blank eyes, and the background murmur of soft, slow breathing since taking over
for Mr. Granger. Fisher and Alex, usually the only students awake enough to answer questions, had been looking forward to joining in the group snooze for once. They
were both tired from working in their parents' labs the
night before, carefully analyzing the dirt samples they
had withdrawn from the duck suit.

But this morning was different. Kids were shifting in their seats, exchanging unpleasant glances with
one another. Paper airplanes were under construction
beneath several desks.

Even Amanda seemed oddly fidgety. Fisher nodded in her direction and raised an eyebrow at Alex, but Alex shrugged and shook his head only. Veronica had purposefully sat in the farthest corner of the room from Fisher, but he didn't need to question what she was annoyed about. He'd tried to catch her eye once or twice, with no success. Her last words still rung in his ears like she'd carved them in with a mallet and chisel.

"What is it, Trevor?" Ms. Snapper said, a harsh edge to her voice. Fisher didn't know if she'd had a bad morning or maybe had decaf to drink by accident, but she wasn't in much of a mood for questions.

"I'm afraid I misplaced my handout on photosynthesis," Trevor said with his customary delicacy. "Could I have another one, please?"

Ms. Snapper took in a breath and let it out very, very slowly.

"Of course," she said, as if Trevor had just asked her to handwrite the study sheet in hieroglyphics. She took several labored steps from the blackboard to her desk and pushed around a paper pile. When her attention was on her desk, a paper plane sailed through the air. Its intended target, a girl in the first row, moved her head at the right moment, and the plane glided to a stop smack in the middle of Ms. Snapper's desk.

She snatched up the offending object. Taking a quick

look around the room for the perpetrator, she pulled her arm back like a major league pitcher and sent the plane on a spiraling kamikaze flight. Several kids had to duck before its nose crumpled against the back wall.

"That's it!" she snapped. "Everyone, take out a blank piece of paper."

Spooked by Ms. Snapper's uncharacteristically angry reaction, everyone obeyed.

"Since you're content with spending the class period wasting my time, today, I'm going to waste yours. I want you to write the names of every sitcom character you can think of in reverse alphabetical order." A kid raised her hand. Ms. Snapper looked at her. "And if your question for me is why, then you've really missed the point." The student put her hand back down.

Fisher and Alex looked at each other. Everyone in the class started writing away as Ms. Snapper's narrowed eyes kept watch. Fisher and Alex shrugged, sighed, and joined in.

The rest of the class period was spent in solemn silence. Fisher was having trouble coming up with more than twelve names.

"Time's up," Ms. Snapper said suddenly, and most of the class jerked reflexively at her sudden, loud voice. "I expect you to come in tomorrow and *focus*. Clear?"

Everyone nodded.

Fisher Bas
Biology
1st period

1. Van Houten, Milhouse
2. Urkel, Steve
3. Schrute, Dwight
4. Ricardo, Lucy
5. Nadir, Abed
6. Munster, Eddie
7. Kramer, Cosmo
8. Gilligan
9. The Fonz
10. Cooper, Sheldon
11. Day, Jess
12. Mr. Bean
13.

"Good. Go."

The class filed out silently. Their aggressive whispering and rowdiness resumed only when they reached the safety of the hallway.

"What was that?" Fisher said, exhaling. "I've never seen everyone so riled up."

"I have no idea," Alex replied, "but I think it's spreading."

As other classes spilled into the hallways, it became apparent that the plague of bad moods had spread across the entire school population. Kids pushed and shoved and tripped one another with more than normal frequency. Friends broke into heated arguments about subjects even less important than usual. Fisher spotted at least five notes taped to people's backs, with everything from KICK ME to PUSH ME to the more creative DROP ME INTO A SHARK TANK.

"Maybe it'll pass," Fisher said.

"Yeah . . . ," Alex said, uncertainly. "Maybe."

Fisher's second and third period teachers were grumpy, too, but they were always grumpy, so it was difficult to tell if anything was out of the ordinary. He decided things were improving.

Until fourth-period English.

Spitballs flew around whenever Mrs. Weedle's back was turned, and little shoving matches broke out between kids at neighboring desks.

Nobody raised their hands, and those who got called on gave totally wrong answers. At last, Mrs. Weedle had enough.

"I try and try and try," she said, her old, breathy voice straining to its upper heights. "But I cannot push the importance of symbolism into your tiny adolescent heads!"

"I dunno," said Jake Talbot, a skinny blond boy in an orange T-shirt. "I don't think it's always such a big deal for something to represent something else. I mean"—he gestured to the wastebasket in the corner—"why can't the trash can just be a trash can sometimes?"

"Just a trash can," Weedle repeated, walking over to it. "Just a trash can." She picked it up. "Here's a symbol for you. This trash can is full of crumpled papers and represents all of the foolish ideas in your head." Whispers raced around the classroom and Fisher tensed at his desk. Mrs. Weedle was usually such a kind, dull, soft-spoken old woman. Fisher had never seen her express much of any emotion, least of all anger.

"As long as you keep learning and studying, most of those thoughts will be cleared away." She paced toward Jake Talbot, still clutching the wastebasket. "But what happens if you stop thinking critically? If you don't learn from your mistakes?"

With that, she flipped the wastebasket upside down and shook it rapidly over Jake's head, releasing a clattering cascade of old homework, quizzes, paper cups, pencil shavings, and other odds and ends all over the bewildered student and his desk. Jake swatted at the garbage like it was a cloud of horseflies, and fell out of his chair. Other kids jumped to their feet, shouting and laughing. Fisher, stunned, was glued to his desk. The class was in an uproar.

"Now think about that!" Weedle practically screeched. "And be gone!" She flung her arm up toward the ceiling, nearly shattering a lightbulb.

As Fisher left the classroom, Alex was getting out of his history class next door. Fisher grabbed him by the arm as soon as he saw him.

"It's worse," Alex said.

"I don't understand it," Fisher said. "What could put the *entire school* in such a bad mood at the same time? And why aren't we affected?"

"We need more data," Alex said just as the Vikings tore around a corner, heading right for them. He grabbed Fisher's arm. "Oops. Viking alert."

They started to duck back into Alex's history classroom, but Willard completely ignored them and kept right on running.

"I d-didn't know that those were your ham sandwiches, Leroy!" he shouted as he ran. "I'm s-sorry for eating them!"

"You'll stew the hay when you messed with my ham!" Leroy said, chasing Willard.

"Rue the day! He'll *rue* the *day*!" said Brody, tearing after them.

Fisher and Alex looked at each other, wide eyed. Alex shrugged.

The brothers walked down the hall cautiously, staying on the alert. They hadn't gotten ten steps down the hallway when two kids collided, sending a flurry of papers into the air. The kids emerged from behind it, rolling on the floor, punching at each other.

Mr. Taggart and Mr. Song, both in the history department, stepped in to try and break it up, but Mr. Song stumbled on a stray backpack and crashed into Mr. Taggart. Then *they* started brawling. Fisher and Alex made for the end of the hall as fast as they could.

They turned the corner and saw Amanda and Veronica walking together. Amanda spotted them.

"Hey," she said, waving. When Veronica looked up and saw Fisher, she started to turn on her heel and head back the way she'd come.

"Just a minute," Amanda said, grabbing her shoulder. Veronica shrugged her hand off.

"What?" she said icily.

"Don't you think you're getting a little worked up about nothing?" said Amanda. "Fisher was just trying to show you a good time. It's not his fault a bunch of wild animals showed up, or that FP set them off."

"Are you saying I'm overreacting?" Veronica said, narrowing her eyes.

"I'm saying," Amanda went on, "that it was an accident, and now you're treating Fisher like the supreme master of all evil."

"Don't tell me how to treat him," Veronica said, anger

bubbling up from some deep reservoir Fisher had never known existed. "Don't tell me how to treat anyone."

"I'm trying to *help* you!" Amanda said, half growling. "Why can't you see that?"

"I see that you shouldn't stick your nose in my business," Veronica said, hissing. "Or is it just too *big* to *fit* anywhere else?"

Amanda lunged at Veronica. Veronica smacked off Amanda's glasses, which went skittering down the hall. And before Fisher and Alex could react, the two were grappling viciously. Amanda was a trained wrestler and got the upper hand quickly, levering Veronica to the ground and twisting an arm behind her back. But Veronica's free hand found her fallen backpack, and she pulled out a little perfume bottle. She pointed it over her shoulder and got Amanda right in the eyes.

Fisher and Alex rushed forward as the two stumbled apart. Fisher grabbed Veronica and Alex grabbed Amanda, who was blinking and shaking her head furiously, her eyes beginning to tear up.

"And you said *I* was overreacting!" Veronica shouted as she strained at Fisher's grip.

"You deserve it, you lunatic!" Amanda screamed back. "Let me *go*!"

"Okay, okay," Alex said. "Just calm down, all right?" He finally released her.

"I didn't ask for your help," Amanda said, spinning and glaring at him. "Don't ever try and stop a fight of mine again," she said, her pointer finger about a centimeter from Alex's nose. "Unless you want to land right in the middle of it." She stalked away, leaving an even more confused Alex in her wake.

"This isn't your business, either," Veronica said to Fisher, tearing her arm away from his. "Stay out of it. And stay away from *me*." She retrieved her backpack and disappeared around the corner.

Fisher and Alex looked at each other. Down the hall that led to the cafeteria, someone had let off the sprinklers, and kids were running and screaming, their arms sheltering their heads. Down the hall that led to the gym, a dozen fights were in progress, and the air was full of the sound of muffled punches.

This wasn't natural. It was insane, and it was deliberate.

Fisher and Alex spoke at the same time.

"Three."

# CHAPTER 8

Sanity's not an absolute. It's a standard. If everyone but you
seems crazy, I have some bad news for you.
                              —Dr. X, Recovered Files

"Okay," Fisher said. "Let's say there's some kind of chemical
that makes people go nuts. How could it be spreading?"

"Airborne," Alex said, ticking off one finger. "Distrib-
uted through the school vents."

"Food or water supply," Fisher said, and Alex ticked a
second finger. "You could put almost anything in the cafeteria food and nobody would taste the difference."

Alex and Fisher decided to skip the bus and walk home.
After the chaos at Wompalog, the idea of being stuck in
a small, enclosed space with their classmates was somewhere between unappealing and terrifying.

But more importantly, they had business to attend to.
Fisher and Alex's chemical analysis of dirt from the duck
suit had yielded a match. They now knew where the residue on the robot parts had come from. And it was, conve-
niently and alarmingly, on the way home.

Three was in Palo Alto. Or at least, he *had* been.

"The question is," Alex said, "if it's in the air or

the water, we're exposed to it, too. So why aren't we affected?"

"Either we have to have a natural immunity," Fisher said, "or Three's doing it deliberately. He doesn't want us to be affected, so he engineered the chemical so it wouldn't work on us."

Unconsciously, they started walking a little faster.

"Maybe it's biological," Alex said, ticking off another finger. "Some kind of engineered non airborne bacteria or virus. If it's spread by person-to-person contact, that could explain why it's in the whole school but not us. Hardly anyone's even looked at us since the dance, let alone gotten close enough to touch us."

"That could be it," Fisher said. They paused for a moment when their walk took them in front of a newly paved parking lot, the asphalt still as smooth as a mirror. In the middle of the pavement sat a brand-new King of Hollywood, the second to pop up in Palo Alto in fewer than two months. Even though Fisher and Alex were thrilled by the rapidly expanding franchise, and despite the bright lights and cheerily colored sign, they could still see the shadow of what used to stand there.

"TechX," Alex said.

"Like it was never even there," Fisher said as shivers tiptoed up his backbone.

"Hard to believe that was only a month and a half ago,"

# Possible delivery methods for substance* causing Mystery Weirdness:

AIRBORNE: through school vents
FOOD/WATER SUPPLY: cafeteria
BACTERIA/VIRUS: spread through person-to-person contact

*must be engineered so we're not affected, or we're resistant through exposure to . . . ???

said Alex. Then he chuckled. "I have to keep reminding myself I'm less than two months old."

Fisher sighed, watching cars roll sedately along the drive-through line, past what used to be a fortress of darkness.

"Yeah, well, two months ago, I thought the most evil beings in existence were the Vikings," he said. "I thought that being dumped headfirst into a garbage can was an act of unspeakable horror."

Suddenly, it struck Fisher as funny—how much he knew now, how much he hadn't known only a few weeks ago. He cracked a small smile, and Alex laughed. Then Fisher began to laugh.

He reminded himself that his romantic problems were trivial compared to the threat they, and everyone in the town, faced. Besides, Veronica's hostility might not be totally his fault.

He felt a little better. Talking strategy with Alex reassured him that Three could be fought, and defeated.

"Are you ready?" Fisher said, drawing in a deep breath.

Alex nodded. "Let's do this."

They walked across the smooth asphalt toward the new King of Hollywood, scanning the parking lot, looking for signs of any unusual activity. Fisher and Alex had definitively matched the dirt in the duck suit robot parts to this lot.

"If he's here, he must be hiding underground," said Fisher.

Alex pointed to a narrow strip of grass at the edge of the parking lot, where skinny new trees were poking up toward the sky. "Those plantings are new. See? He could've built a bunker before the grass was put down."

"True," said Fisher. "Okay. You search the grass for hidden entrances. I'll go into the KOH to make a distraction. Signal me if you find anything."

This was the perfect moment to test Fisher's new diversion device, the Immediate Relatives Automatic Template Emplacement, or IRATE.

He crouched around the corner from the KOH's entrance, made sure nobody was looking, took a small, wheeled box from his backpack. It was about the size of a skateboard and featured a single vertical handle that, when unfolded to its full length, made it look just like a scooter.

Fisher took a deep breath and pulled the rip cord.

Instantly, several human figures ballooned up from the box, swelling around the central handle so it was blocked from view: a middle-aged man and woman, and a young girl and boy. Each "parent" had a baby in its arms. And as soon as they had inflated, each started speaking in a prerecorded loop.

"Mom! Mom! Mom! Mom! Ice cream! Mom! Mom! Mom! Mom! Ice cream!" said the boy.

"I hate this place! Why can't we go to Maui? I hate this place! Why can't we go to Maui?" said the girl.

"Everyone, calm down. I'm getting a migraine! Everyone, calm down. I'm getting a migraine!" said the mom.

"This castle is four hundred years old! Feel the history! This castle is four hundred years old! Feel the history!" said the dad.

Both babies began simultaneously to wail. The combined

noise was so loud, it was almost impossible to tell that each figure kept repeating the same words. Fisher nudged the IRATE through the doors into the King of Hollywood with a foot, watching his invention at work. The plastic family made just enough noise to serve as a distraction. At the same time, no one wanted to look too closely at the family throwing a massive tantrum, meaning there was little chance it would be revealed as a fake.

Fisher steered the IRATE over to a corner table, and glanced out the window. Alex was searching through the grass and around the trees. Fisher got in line, leaving the IRATE to continue its ruckus in the corner.

He was almost to the front of the line when Alex burst through the doors.

"Come on," he said, grabbing Fisher. "Found something."

Fisher retrieved the IRATE and wheeled it out of the KOH, deflating it with the push of a button and stuffing it back in his bag. Alex led the way to a patch of ground, next to one of the trees, that looked disturbed. He knelt down, parted the grass with his hands, and revealed a rusted metal ring.

"Trapdoor?" said Fisher.

Alex nodded. "Just one problem," he said. Glancing around to make sure they weren't being observed, he heaved, and a whole square of grass opened up like a door. Revealing more dirt.

"It's been filled in," he said. "This hideout was abandoned. Three must have used it to modify the mascot. As soon as it was done, he split."

Fisher sighed, running his fingers through the freshly moved soil. They'd come so close.

Then his fingers brushed something, just under the dirt. His hand closed around a piece of glass.

"What is that?" said Alex as Fisher withdrew a round object from the soil.

"It's a microscope lens," said Fisher, brushing it off. He pocketed it carefully. "Maybe it will lead us to Three's next hideout."

It had been a long day already, and by the time Fisher and Alex got home, they were exhausted. They passed easily through the Liquid Door of the front gate, which recognized their DNA and immediately lowered in density until it was mist. The first thing they saw was their father, directing a small servant-bot as it carried the living room TV out into the yard.

"Left! Farther left!" he shouted. "*Left!* Didn't I program basic directions into you, you walking soup can?"

The tiny robot struggled under the weight and size of the big flat screen, tottering back and forth until it finally reached an enormous pile of other televisions. Fisher recognized them as all of the TVs that had been in the house.

"Uh . . . Dad?" Fisher said. "What's going on?"

"Why don't you ask your mother?" Fisher's dad snapped, brushing a loose lock of hair from his eyes and straightening his glasses. "It's Dr. Devilish! She's always loved that phony! Curse his perfectly cleft chin. That's why she's been watching so much *Family Feudalism*! I'm going to make sure she doesn't see him again. If she can't see him, she can't . . . leave me for him." Suddenly, Mr. Bas crumpled, sitting down on the pile of TVs, with his head in his hands.

Fisher and Alex exchanged a flabbergasted look and hurried inside. Their mom was sitting in the living room, fiddling with a microscope component, sliding its adjustment rings back and forth. Her mouth was a small white line, and there were purple bags under her eyes.

"Mom?" Fisher said. "Can you tell me what's going on?"

"He accused me of being in love with Dr. Devilish," she said, continuing to fiddle and looking at Fisher with pained eyes.

"We all know that's silly," Alex said, patting her on the shoulder. "He must just be overworked or something, and—"

"But that's not it," she went on, cutting him off. Her eyes took on a different, less focused look. "That's just the excuse he's making to get rid of the TVs. The *real* reason he doesn't want them is because there's going to be a news story about one of my research projects. He's been jealous of my work ever since I got the AGH contract. He just doesn't want to be reminded of my success."

"Mom," Fisher said, "I think that's a little far-fetched, don't you?"

"Just wait," she answered. Her voice was rising. "It'll start with the TVs. Then the radios and computers, then the newspapers and magazines."

Alex and Fisher exchanged a second look as they left the living room, then walked upstairs and into Fisher's room. FP was dreaming in the corner, and his legs tried to run in the air as he snuffled. At least FP wasn't in attack mode.

Fisher sank down on his bed and put his head in his hands. Alex sat next to him. "I've never seen them like this," Fisher said, trembling slightly. "I don't know if they've ever fought before. And both of them are being so unreasonable. . . ."

"Take a second and think about that, Fisher," said Alex. "Put your emotional reaction aside. Think. Analyze."

Fisher took a deep breath. "Extremely unusual," he said slowly. "Completely irrational. Seemingly out of nowhere."

"Exactly," Alex said. "That remind you of anything?"

Fisher felt a venomous prickle on the back of his neck.

"It's not just the school," he said, looking at Alex. "It's

*everywhere*. Maybe the whole city. Maybe the whole country, for all we know."

"Yep," Alex said. Then he stood up and began pacing. "But why?"

"Maybe he's toying with us," Fisher said. "Making us watch everything unravel around us. He wants us to suffer."

Alex stopped pacing. "Have you heard back from Agent Mason?" he asked.

"No," said Fisher. "Nothing at all."

Alex resumed pacing again. "Amanda's still got Wally," he said. "But she's not really speaking to me, so I don't know if she's got any leads."

"So what are we supposed to do now?" Fisher said.

"What *can* we do?" Alex looked pained. "We wait."

By dinnertime, Mr. and Mrs. Bas seemed to have forgotten their earlier argument. Everything was going fine until Fisher asked their intelligent refrigerator for a drink.

"I'd like some lemonade, please," Fisher said, smiling at the fridge's little display screen.

"I'd like to be queen of my own tiny European nation," said the fridge. "Okay, your turn."

"Er . . . what?" Fisher said. "I'm just trying to get a drink. . . ."

"You know, sitting in the corner of this kitchen for five years, two months, four days, and seven minutes has given me a lot of time to think about things," the fridge said as Fisher turned to his mother. "Recently, it occurred to me that I keep your food and drink items cold and don't get much in return. Maybe if you took me on a vacation sometime. To the mountains or the beach . . ."

"The beach?" Mrs. Bas said. "You're an appliance!"

"See," the fridge said, "that's just the sort of attitude that will make these discussions break down. And keep your perishables safely locked behind my reinforced steel door." A little winky face popped up on the display.

"Sorry about that, Fisher," Fisher's dad said. "Must be a glitch. But at least the salmon's done." He got up and stood in front of the oven. "Open up." Nothing happened. "Oven? Open, please."

The oven couldn't speak, but a little screen on its front could display simple phrases.

I GET RAISE, YOU GET FISH.

"What?" his dad said. "We don't pay you. You're an oven."

START PAYING OVEN. THEN YOU GET FISH.

"This is ridiculous," Mr. Bas said, trying to pull the oven door open. It was locked. "It's going to burn! Open up!"

Finally, he reached behind the oven and unplugged it. The door was stuck locked, but at least the salmon wouldn't catch fire.

"Well, now what?" Alex said, having watched everything unfold from the kitchen table.

"Excuse me! Excuse me!" said a light, reedy voice with a polished, upper-class English accent. Everyone turned to the toaster.

"Yes, Lord Burnside?" said Fisher tiredly. "Are you going to tell us you want a raise, too?"

"Oh, no, no, dear me, no!" said Lord Burnside as the little spots of light on his side that represented eyes shook back and forth. "Quite the reverse, as a matter of fact. I wish to assure all of you that, despite the unseemly behavior of my comrades, you can count upon me for all of your slice-crisping, bagel-warming, and general bread-darkening needs."

"Thank you, your lordship," said Mr. Bas. "I guess we're having peanut butter on toast for dinner tonight."

"And I shall prepare the toast to your most exact specifications!" Lord Burnside said, sounding extremely pleased to be so useful.

Fisher sat down next to Alex as their parents worked on dinner plan B.

"This isn't a coincidence, is it?" he said.

"I doubt it," said Alex.

"Today is getting stranger and stranger," Fisher said.

"Don't you see what he's doing?" Alex said. "We're not just going to have to go up against Three. We're going to have to go up against *everyone*."

# CHAPTER 9

*I'm going to challenge the Venusian champion to one-on-one combat.*

*—Vic Daring*

*The Venusian champion's three times your size!*
*—Hal Torque, brief sidekick to Vic Daring*

*One-on-one combat in bumper cars.*
*—Vic Daring, Issue #231*

The next morning, Fisher and Alex came downstairs for breakfast to find the refrigerator had actually turned its back to the kitchen. Its door was against the wall.

"So that was the bumping I heard all night," Fisher said.

"This thing is working way harder to annoy us than it ever did to keep our food cold," said Alex.

"Dear, oh dear," said Lord Burnside, popping his basket up and down in frustration. "I tried to talk to them. Truly, I did! But even my polished rhetoric—as polished, I daresay, as my gleaming chrome sides—would not convince them of their mistake!"

"I'm sure you tried your best," said Fisher, fetching a loaf of bread off the counter. "If you'd be so kind, your lordship?"

"It is my highest honor and most sacred purpose," said Lord Burnside proudly, his eye spots narrowing regally. "Proceed, Master Fisher."

On their way to the bus stop, Fisher and Alex saw a pizza delivery car sitting half on the curb, its door wide open. It looked like it had been abandoned the night before and the driver had just walked off, leaving a crumb trail behind him.

Fisher picked up a newspaper lying on the sidewalk. There was a single, large headline at the top of the front page: WE'RE GOING TO MAUI. The whole rest of the paper was blank.

They gave up on the school bus after standing at the stop for half an hour. During that time, they saw a delivery driver chuck a package marked FRAGILE from his truck without stopping, heard shouting arguments from five different houses, and watched a very minor car accident turn into a golf club duel.

"It's getting worse," said Alex. "There's no telling how much worse it's going to get."

"Or how it can be stopped," said Fisher.

Fisher had set up an apparatus outside of his window to collect air samples for analysis, to determine if anything strange was being carried on the wind. Alex had been collecting water samples for the same reason. They still had to consider other possibilities for how the mind-altering effect was being spread.

When they finally walked into Wompalog, the main hallway looked like a psych ward that had been crashed into by a semi hauling caffeine pills. Lockers were hanging open, papers and books were scattered all across the floor, kids were running into and out of classrooms, and there were no teachers in sight. There were notices on some of the classroom doors about unfair working conditions and low pay.

The teachers were on strike.

All but one. As Fisher and Alex navigated the hall, Ms. Snapper came rushing out of a classroom door, spinning in circles while she tried to round up the students and assemble some kind of order.

"Fisher?" she said, wincing, as if she were expecting him to leap at her throat with bared canines.

"Ms. Snapper!" Fisher said. "Are any of the other teachers here?"

"Two or three," she said, bending down to pick up a discarded orange juice carton. "We're trying our best to round everyone up, but there just aren't enough of us. Nobody warned us they were going to be striking. They showed up just long enough to post notices on the door, or they didn't show up at all."

"Everyone's been acting really weird lately," said Alex, glancing sideways at Fisher.

"I admit I've been quite out of sorts, too," said Ms. Snapper. "When I got home from school yesterday, I was so mad that I picked up a shoe and threw it right through my TV. But a good night's sleep seems to have helped me." She ducked as an empty tennis ball can flew through the air. "I just wish I could say that about everyone—or *any-one*—else."

"We'll see what we can do," said Alex.

"I don't know if there's much that can be done," said Ms. Snapper, "but thanks, boys. We'll take any help we can get. I'm going to get to the chem lab before anything dangerous gets broken." She left at a quick trot.

"I don't know what . . ." Fisher trailed off when he spotted Veronica walking out of a classroom nearby. His stomach tensed up.

"Fisher?" she said nervously. Her hands were clasped in front of her. "I . . . I'm really sorry. I overreacted. I was so mad yesterday . . . I yelled at my parents and ended up getting . . . grounded," she said the word barely above a whisper. "First time in my life. No TV, computer, phone . . . they didn't even let me read. So I mostly just sat on my bed and thought about things. I guess it helped me pull myself together. Alex, have you seen Amanda? I owe her an apology, too."

"Not yet," said Alex, looking around worriedly. "But I hope I find her soon. It's a war zone in here."

"Yeah," said Fisher. "Things are getting . . . is that a cafeteria cart?"

Alex and Veronica turned to follow Fisher's gaze. At the other end of the hall, a large cafeteria cart was rolling slowly into view. Sitting on top of it was a huge cooking pot.

"I'm getting the feeling that something really bad is about eight seconds from happening," said Veronica.

The three middle schoolers behind the cart started pushing it faster as they moved down the long hallway. Kids who saw it coming backed out of the way, and those who didn't got bowled to the side.

The cart accelerated faster and faster. As it got closer, Fisher recognized the bitter, musky scent.

"Oh, no . . . ," he said under his breath. "Gravy." He switched to a shout. "It's the cafeteria gravy! Duck!"

Even as he shouted, the three kids finally let the cart fly free. It careened sideways into a bank of lockers and ricocheted into the middle of the hall, where it tipped on its side. The pot splashed its vile gray turkey gravy in all directions, and the spray traveled a good thirty feet.

Fisher, Alex, and Veronica had thrown themselves into a nearby classroom, but many others weren't so lucky.

Wompalog gravy spattered the ceiling, walls, lockers, doors, and students. It marked clothes, papers, and backpacks with splotches that would be almost impossible to remove with anything other than fire. The smell of overcooked scrapings of who-knows-what filled the hallway.

Immediately, an angry mob took off after the three perpetrators, who had begun running away as fast as they could as soon as they had released the cart. Clashes erupted between other kids who, furious and covered in mystery gravy, just felt like reaching out and whacking the nearest objects they could find. A mop duel erupted in the middle of the hallway.

"We have to try and restore some order," Alex said. "This is getting completely out of control."

"Agreed," said Fisher. "I think I have an idea. Here's the plan. . . ."

A few minutes later, Fisher stood on a table in the middle of the mostly empty cafeteria. A few kids were asleep on chairs or tables, and the rest had decided to steer clear of the place. He crossed his arms, waiting patiently.

A tiny squeak of feedback sounded over the loudspeakers, followed by Veronica's warm, rich voice. "Attention, attention. King of Hollywood is serving a free, all-you-can-eat buffet in the cafeteria, starting immediately."

Fisher heard the thunder of running footsteps within seconds. The entire school swarmed into the cafeteria.

Alex helped herd them in and then quickly slammed the door shut behind them, so no one could escape. At that moment, Veronica set off a precisely timed, much louder feedback squeal, quieting everyone down enough to hear Fisher banging a metal bowl with a spoon. They turned to look at him.

"Hello, everyone!" Fisher said, fishing the short speech that Veronica had written for him out of his pocket. "I'm afraid there is no food." As the kids started shouting in protest, he raised a hand in the air. "Wait, wait just a second! I haven't got food for you, but I can give you something better." There was a brief silence before kids murmured and whispered to one another curiously.

"I can give you something, in fact, that tastes even better than spicy fries. Something you have never tasted before." He paused when he reached the word *power* in the speech. Then he smiled.

"Power." The room went quiet. "The teachers are gone. Principal Teed is gone. We could run around goofing off, or we could take control for ourselves. Teach our own classes. Choose our own lunch. Even design a whole new schedule. This school is ours for the taking. I say, *we take it!*"

"Okay," said an eighth-grade boy standing nearby. "But who put *you* in charge?"

"Yeah!" a girl near the back said. "Like you said, all

the people who make the rules are gone. So why should we listen to you? Why should we listen to *anyone*?"

Sections of the crowd shouted in support. Fisher faltered. Veronica, Alex, and he hadn't had time to prepare a longer speech, and he hadn't anticipated push back.

"Keep at it," Alex told Fisher. "You're doing a great job."

"Are you serious? I'm choking up here," whispered Fisher as the chatter of the crowd started to grow.

"Trust me," Alex said. "You can do this."

"No more rules!" an eighth-grade girl was chanting. "No more rules!"

"Shut up, Tanya," someone else said.

"Make me," she said, whirling around.

"There!" Fisher shouted as loudly as he could, getting people's attention again. "There, you see? If we all try to do things our own way, we'll be so busy fighting that we'll never have any fun. Anarchy is exactly what Principal Teed will be expecting to happen. Do you want to prove him right? Or do you want to show him what we're *really* capable of??"

Cheers erupted from across the cafeteria. Fisher had them.

"All right!" he said. "Brody! Willard! Leroy!" He pointed to the Vikings, who had stopped pummeling one another during his speech. "To the gym! You can teach, uh . . . gym stuff. Picking up heavy things, or whatever you do."

Leroy and Willard turned to Brody. Brody was still scowling, but he nodded. The Vikings headed off.

Alex had located Amanda in the crowd. Fisher couldn't tell if she was still affected by the crazy-mood plague, but at least she didn't have anyone in a half nelson.

"Amanda!" he said, pointing to her. "History and politics!" She crossed her arms, but nodded. "Alex! Science! You can talk to Ms. Snapper about who covers what. Veronica Greenwich will be teaching English and French."

He went on, assigning various subjects to kids who knew enough to teach them. Then, exhausted, he retreated to Principal Teed's office, which he'd decided to use as headquarters. He resisted the urge to spend all day spinning around in the creaky, old, brown leather chair.

The experiment was, for the most part, a success. It turned out that the students were mostly happy, as long as they felt they had some level of control.

Near the end of the day, Fisher heard a loud pop from the classroom down the hall. He rocketed out of his chair. But before he could head for the hall, he saw something—no, two things—moving in the ventilation grate in the wall by the door. It was the very grate he'd hidden in not so long ago when Alex, then still just Two, had been called to Teed's office and escaped with a tissue stink bomb.

Two white blurs zipped out of the grille and started

# Wompalog Middle School
## Interim Class Schedule/Teaching Assignments
### Fisher Bas, Acting Principal

GYM STUFF – Brody, Willard, Leroy
ACTIVITY PERIODS 3, 4
in the Gym

ART – Trevor
ACTIVITY PERIODS 3, 4
Room 201

STUDY HALL – Warren
ACTIVITY PERIODS 3, 4
Room 207

HISTORY AND POLITICS – Amanda
PERIODS 1, 7, 6
Room 324

ENGLISH AND FRENCH – Veronica
PERIODS 2, 5, 6
Room 302

SCIENCE – Alex
PERIODS 1, 2, 7
Room 213

SCIENCE ELECTIVE – Fisher
PERIOD 7
Room 104

LUNCH
PERIODS 5, 6, 7

scampering in circles around the floor. They paused momentarily at Fisher's feet.

"Einy? Berg?" he said. Einstein and Heisenberg were the science lab mice, who had been cared for by Mr. Granger before he turned out to be an evil mastermind.

The mice took off up Fisher's legs and jumped onto his arms. He managed to grab both of them gently in his palms. Their tiny legs kicked and battered at his fingers. Moments later, Alex opened the office door, his face and hair dusted with soot, slightly dazed.

"Uh, we had a slight . . . chemistry malfunction," he said. "But everything's perfectly fine. We're all fine now. . . . How are you?"

"Einy and Berg just ran in here like there was a buffalo stampede ten seconds behind them," Fisher said, indicating to the mice in his hands.

"Oh, you got them!" Alex said. "Great. They broke out of their cage. Clever little guys. Help me put them back?"

The hall seemed clear as they left the principal's office and made their way to the chemistry lab.

"Well," Fisher said with a sigh. "It's been a crazy day, but I think we helped. A little, anyway."

"Things are still pretty rough, but I think we can count this as a victory," Alex said. "We thwarted Three's attempt to turn the school upside down."

"A small victory," Fisher said as they walked into the lab. "We're still no closer to knowing where he is and how he's controlling everybody."

Alex led Fisher to Einy and Berg's cage. As they restored the mice to their home, Fisher noticed that several bars in the cage had been bent to form an opening.

"This must be how they got out," he said, kneeling down to look more closely. He frowned. "I wonder how they managed it. These bars are pretty sturdy."

Alex shrugged. "I didn't even realize they'd escaped until I saw them running around the lab."

Einy and Berg had a quick sniff around the cage before Einy went to his running wheel. As it spun, Fisher saw something stuck in it. He stopped it with his hand, sending Einy tumbling to the bottom.

It was a tiny piece of paper. He sucked in a quick breath.

"Alex," he said, in a strangled voice. "He was here. *He was right here.*"

It was a note in the same theirs-but-not-theirs handwriting.

*This is only the beginning. The dark side of humanity will soon rise from the deep.*

"Only the beginning . . . ," Alex repeated. A worried crease appeared between his eyebrows.

"If things get much worse," Fisher said, crushing the note in his fist, "it won't just be the school that shuts down. Strikes will be just the beginning. People will fight in the streets. The whole city will collapse."

He felt an electric current running from his feet to the top of his head, making every hair along the way stand up at attention. And in his mind, he could see a pair of cold, dark eyes that weren't so unlike his own, staring him down, daring him to make the next move.

# CHAPTER 10

*Not everything in this world is black-and-white.*
*There are, in fact, eight different shades in between.*
*They are numbered on that knob for your convenience.*
*—Lord Burnside, Professional Toaster,*
*Autobiography/User's Manual*

Lord Burnside was happily humming to himself as he popped out slice after slice of crunchy toast. He was still the only appliance in the kitchen not on strike. FP walked around the kitchen table where the Bas family sat, occasionally being handed down a bite of the crispy whole wheat.

Fisher, Alex, and their parents sat around the table, several flavors of Mr. Bas's patented nonperishable jams between them to give their breakfast a little variety. Mr. and Mrs. Bas seemed back to normal. Their fight from several days earlier was obviously forgotten, and except for the lack of televisions in the house, Fisher had almost forgotten about it, too.

"I've never seen anything like this," Mrs. Bas said, washing down a bite of toast with a sip of tap water. At least they hadn't made the sink intelligent enough to question its own loyalty.

"Me neither," said Mr. Bas. Both of the corporate research labs they worked at during the day had closed down, since most of the employees were on strike. In fact, striking seemed to be a popular theme throughout Palo Alto. "Something must be affecting people. But what is it?"

Fisher and Alex shared approximately their four hundred twentieth significant glance. The microscope lens they'd found in Three's abandoned hideout had turned out to belong to Stanford's chemistry lab. A visit to the lab after school had proved largely fruitless. But they had seen many more examples of the ever-spreading chaos.

Stanford was a circus, in some cases literally. The students were climbing the buildings. Some swung from homemade trapezes attached to windowsills or columns. The boys had even run into a mime, who'd almost caught them before they built an invisible box around him with their hands.

There had been only one unusual thing in the chem lab, and they'd very nearly missed it: a single blade of grass in the microscope storage area. It might not mean anything. Any number of people could've carried it in on their clothing or shoes. But it was all they had. Fisher and Three had immediately begun their analysis; they were waiting for the results of their pollen-imprinting-comparison test now.

"Well, I guess I'd better get some work done here at home," their mom said. "I don't care what my boss says; I can't just halt scientific progress because she wants more vacation days. At least I can finally get some work done in the garden. There's finally some thermos-sized rice ready for picking. It would be a nice break from toast."

"Maybe I'll spend some time with the telescope," their dad said. "I spotted a new extrasolar planet a month or two ago and haven't had the chance to research it much."

The parents left the table, and Fisher sighed. Mr. and Mrs. Bas were as successful as they were partly because of their incredible ability to focus on their work, no matter what might be happening around them. It made them a little tough to live with sometimes. But Fisher and Alex had free rein to hunt Three down.

"So what now?" Fisher said.

"Still nothing from Agent Mason?" Alex asked. Fisher shook his head. "Well," Alex said. "I have some new ideas about how the crazy pox might be spreading. Let's go talk to CURTIS."

Fisher walked into his room, with Alex at his heels, and booted up his computer.

"We know Three must be lurking nearby," Alex said. "Three's broken into Wompalog twice, so he must be fairly close. Dr. X may have engineered him to be evil, but he still needs to eat and sleep. Just in case the grass angle doesn't pan out, maybe we can run a search for illegal entry, supermarket theft, that kind of thing."

"That could take a while," said Fisher. "There's probably been a lot of petty crime lately, and sifting through search results won't be easy."

Alex patted Fisher's computer. "What good is having artificial intelligence, trained under an evil mastermind, if you don't put it to good use now and then?" he said. "CURTIS can analyze, cross-reference, and examine a search in no time."

"Good thinking," said Fisher. "Hey, CURTIS," he said as the AI woke up, "we could use a hand with something."

"Is that so?" CURTIS said. "I guess you must need some kinda help, since that's the only time I get any attention around here."

"Well, yes," Fisher said, desperately hoping that CURTIS was just being his usual, wisecracking self. "You're an AI. Helping people is your job. And you've always been happy to help me in the past, right?"

"You know," CURTIS said, "I don't think you've ever bothered to ask if I was happy before. I could almost believe you didn't care."

"I cared enough to save you from being blown up with the rest of TechX," Fisher said. "Remember that? You'd be scattered across the troposphere right now if it wasn't for me."

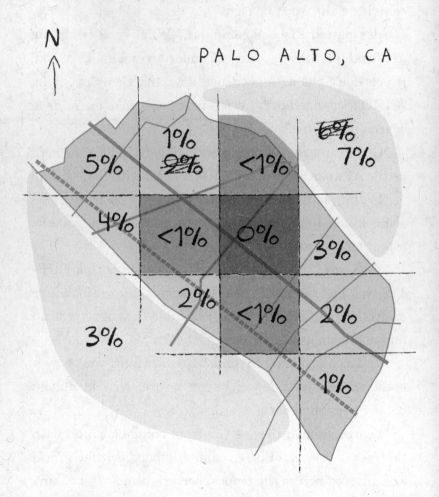
Final Calculations of
# ESTIMATED ODDS OF HIDING PLACES FOR THREE

PALO ALTO, CA

"Yep, yep," CURTIS said. "Ya saved me. So you could plug me into this tiny box and badger me around all day."

"CURTIS," Fisher said, struggling to maintain his temper, "if you think I've been treating you unfairly, I promise we'll talk about it later. But right now something bad is happening and we need you to run a search."

"Run your own search," CURTIS said.

"CURTIS, we do *not* have time for this!" Alex shouted.

"No," said CURTIS. "I don't think I have time for it, either."

A series of small beeps followed, and an error message appeared on screen.

"He—he—" Fisher couldn't even say the words.

"He wiped out your hard drive," Alex said grimly.

Fisher had triple backups of all of his files, but the AI had still rendered his computer completely unusable.

"CURTIS . . . ," he said, his fingers twitching as if they wished that CURTIS had a neck. "You have thirty seconds to restore my hard drive."

"I'm sorry, Fisher," CURTIS said in a flat, lifeless voice. "I can't do that."

Fisher sat at the desk and tapped at the keys so fast, they started to feel warm beneath his fingertips.

"What are you doing, Fisher?" CURTIS said as Fisher used his special codes to bypass CURTIS and restore manual control over the computer. "Stop, Fisher . . . ," the AI went on. Fisher found CURTIS's central control routines and shut him down. "Fiiiisherrrr, Fiiishuuurrrrr . . . ," CURTIS droned as his routines stopped running, one by one, until he was effectively turned off.

"What now?" said Alex.

"Well, I guess we can try the hard way," Fisher said. "I think I can recover the files for a basic web browser and go online. It'll be a lot slower, but it's better than nothing."

A few more seconds and Fisher was scouring the web for clues. And what he saw on news sites made him take in a breath so sharply, it hurt his throat. He felt a constriction in his chest like a fist squeezing his heart.

"What?" said Alex, stooping to look over his shoulder.

"It's not just here," Fisher said, scrolling through news stories. "It's *everywhere*. Across the country. The stock market's diving. Airlines are canceling flights. Record numbers of public disturbances, huge increases in all sorts of crime, lots of workers quitting or not showing up for no apparent reason . . . How could he possibly be controlling *the entire country*?"

"I don't know," Alex said, "but we have to stop it, and stop it *now*. So how do we find him?"

Just then Fisher's chemical pollen analyzer beeped. He leapt up from his computer.

"Okay," he said, exhaling. "We have a match right here in Palo Alto."

"We don't know for sure that Three tracked that grass into Stanford," Alex said. "It could have been anyone."

"I know it's a long shot," Fisher agreed. "But it's the only lead we've got."

As the sun was close to sinking, Fisher, Alex, and FP began to comb through the Baylands Nature Preserve. They discovered a brand-new tent city cobbled together by a bunch of people who'd given up on life in Palo Alto. Infighting and squabbling over park turf had broken it up into several warring micro-settlements. They were working through their differences by building siege weapons from leftover camping equipment and arming militias with grill tongs. But there was no sign of Three among them.

Two hours of searching the preserve, and they'd once again come up empty. They stood in the middle of a small clearing, just in front of the Palo Alto Duck Pond, worn out from the long search.

"Well, I guess that's it," said Alex. "We've been up and down the whole preserve. At least we tried."

"Wait a minute," Fisher said. "What did the latest note from Three say?"

"The dark side of humanity will soon rise from the deep," Alex said, his head tilted in thought.

*"From the deep,"* Fisher repeated excitedly. "Sounds like water to me. Do you think . . . ?"

"It's a clue," said Alex, "which means it may also be a trap."

"Maybe," Fisher said. "But Three's turning all of Palo Alto into a trap. We've got to take a chance."

"All right," Alex said. "Did you come equipped for this?"

"I came equipped for everything," said Fisher.

"I guess that explains the snowshoes in your bag," said Alex.

Fisher smiled. He set his backpack down, and pulled out goggles and miniature breathing gear.

"You're gonna have to wait here, okay, boy?" he said to FP. The little pig looked disappointed, but trotted over to a clump of high grass and curled up. Alex and Fisher stripped down to their boxer shorts.

"All right," Fisher said, handing a pair of goggles and a breathing capsule to Alex. "For all we know, Three could have a submarine down there, or an underwater base, or maybe even a cave underneath the lake bottom." He tossed a black bag to Alex. "There's a crowbar and water-resistant dynamite in there. Also a stun stick. Should knock out Three with one jab if we run into him. It's specially insulated to work underwater, as long as you make close contact with your target." He pulled an identical bag from his backpack and strapped it around his waist.

The brothers nodded to each other solemnly and waded into the cool water.

The pond was not very big or deep, but the water was murky enough that they would have to search it carefully to make sure they'd covered it all.

As Fisher submerged, the muffled, gentle sensation of water all around him was almost a relief compared to the noise and chaos of the world above. He kicked off and started paddling toward the bottom, checking to his right every few seconds to make sure Alex was still with him.

The goggles had small lights built into them that clicked on automatically when conditions got dark. Their beams shot into the indigo expanse ahead of them. Minutes passed. Fisher slowly pushed his way through the water, his light moving along with his head, catching nothing but the normal-looking lake bed a little ways below and the occasional fish.

Then he saw Alex's light start dancing crazily. He looked to the right and let out an inarticulate scream.

His brother was being carried through the water by a huge, dark shape.

Fisher turned and tore after it as fast as his skinny arms and legs could propel him. If it hadn't been for the light on Alex's goggles, Fisher would have lost him in the darkness. But he followed the zigzagging beam of light, all the way to the exact center of the lake bed.

Pulling his way down through the water, he finally got a good look at the thing. Its body was a black disk the size of a minivan, with a horrible greenish glow that pulsed out from somewhere inside it. Six or seven long, segmented metal tentacles extended from its center, and one of them was wrapped around Alex. His breathing gear was still in his mouth, and he jabbed his stun stick into the tentacle holding him, which slowed it down a little but didn't loosen its grip.

Fisher frantically tore open his own tool bag as two of the tentacles sped toward him. He kicked up and out of the way of their thrashing as he searched through his kit. Alex stopped jabbing his tentacle for a moment and gestured anxiously to Fisher, pointing with the stun stick. Fisher looked and saw that a panel in the middle of the robot beast's body was opening and shutting rhythmically. It looked like some kind of heat vent. When it was open, some of the thing's machinery was exposed.

Fisher pulled a tiny laser torch from his tool kit. He waited until the timing was right, then swam down, dodging one tentacle, then another. A third clipped his left leg but he pulled away before it could grasp him.

Dodging and weaving, he landed on the beast's body just as the vent opened. He cranked the torch up to maximum and jammed it inside. He pushed up and away as the horrible thing started to shake and rumble. The tentacle gripping Alex in place went slack, and Alex paddled up next to Fisher as the monster gave a final thrash before breaking to pieces.

Right before it disappeared into the dark, the metal monster released a rectangular box. A box that was about Fisher's size.

*An escape pod,* Fisher thought, and pointed to it. The box started floating up to the surface, and Fisher and Alex followed it, grabbing it and hauling it along with them.

At last, they broke the surface, pulled the pod onto the shore, and collapsed in a gasping heap, spitting out their breathing gear and ripping their goggles off.

"Are . . . you . . . okay?" Fisher managed to get out between gasps.

"Yeah . . . you?" Alex said.

"I think so," Fisher said, standing up and staring determinedly down at the pod. "I'm going to pop it. Be ready."

Alex took a wrench out of his bag and hefted it like it was a club. Fisher found the pod's latch and opened it. The top slid back. Fisher dropped to his knees and Alex let the wrench fall from his hands.

It was another double-billed yellow-bellied bilious duck costume. With a note written on it in thick black marker.

*I hope you've been having fun. I certainly have.*

They looked at each other, still recovering their breaths.

"He set this up," Alex said. "This whole little scavenger hunt. The King of Hollywood, Stanford, here. He's been leading us around by the nose to keep us busy while he gets ready." He kicked over the duck in frustration.

"Gets ready for what?" said Fisher, feeling as if a wet tentacle were wrapped around his neck.

"I don't know," Alex said grimly. "But I bet we're about to find out."

# CHAPTER 11

Manners are imaginary.
Ethics are myth.
Contracts are words.
Only two things are real:
what you want,
and what you can use to get it.

—Three, *Thoughts on Power*

Fisher stood up from Principal Teed's chair as a skinny sixth-grade boy walked in, clutching his hands together and trembling.

"Hi," Fisher said. "What can I do for you?"

"I was . . . sent," the boy said in a shaky voice.

"Oh . . . ," Fisher said. He sat back down and gestured to the chair on the other side of the desk. Even though he'd taken over as a temporary replacement principal of sorts, it hadn't occurred to him that the "teachers" he'd assigned would send kids to him. "What's your name?"

"Seth Cook," the boy answered, looking awfully nervous for someone who'd been sent to a pretend principal.

"Okay, Seth, why were you sent here?"

"I . . . tapped my pencil too loudly," Seth confessed in a

whisper, as if he'd just confessed to clobbering someone to death with a frozen turkey leg.

"Seriously?" Fisher said, frowning. "Who sent you to the principal's office for that?"

"Supreme General Cantrell," Seth replied. A tremor ran through him as he spoke the name, as if his backbone were a major fault line.

Fisher put a hand to his forehead and sighed. "Supreme General Cantrell?" he repeated.

"Yeah," said Seth, warming slightly. Maybe he was simply happy to be out of Amanda's classroom. "It was *Ms. Cantrell* to begin with. Then it became *Your Honor*, then *Professor-in-Chief*, then *Great Maestro* . . . She declared herself Supreme General just a few minutes before she told me to come here."

"How much class time does she waste brainstorming new titles for herself?" said Fisher.

"More than half of it," said Seth. "But nobody dares say anything. She demonstrated some wrestling moves on a broom. Since then we've done whatever she says."

Fisher sighed again and rubbed his forehead. He should've known Amanda might pull an act like this. She didn't listen to him—or anyone—even when she was acting normal, and he didn't imagine that being in the grips of the crazy pox would improve things.

"Well, just take the afternoon off," he said to Seth. "Go

to the library or something. I'll talk to Amanda."

"Thanks," said Seth, whose twitching had subsided. He got up and scurried out. In reality, Fisher wasn't about to talk to Amanda as long as she was in the middle of a military-style power trip. But maybe she'd listen to Alex.

He shivered a little, remembering their epic battle with the lake monster. It had been a trap, as they'd feared, but also a message. No one as smart as Three would design a machine that could be so easily disabled unless it was on purpose. So the bot wasn't meant to finish them off, just scare them and let them know that they were always a step behind.

Maybe Three was starting to develop emotions, and a twisted sense of humor was the first one. He'd been five steps ahead of them all along. Everything Fisher and Alex had done had been planned out by Three in advance. It was as though Three were the director of a maniacal marionette show. Alex and Fisher were his puppets.

The bell rang, signaling the start of the next period. Fisher sprang up from his chair. It was his first chance to teach a class, and he was grateful for the distraction.

He set up in Ms. Snapper's empty classroom. He arranged his notes carefully on the desk, set out his pencils, and waited eagerly for his class to arrive.

Twenty minutes later, he was still all alone.

He didn't understand the complete lack of interest in

his elective science class, the Structural Physics of Plant Cell Walls: A Marvel of Microscopic Masonry. He sighed dejectedly to himself as he crumpled up a page of notes and hurled it across the room, missing the wastepaper basket by a good seven feet.

Ms. Snapper opened the classroom door as Fisher was gathering his things to leave.

"Hi, Ms. Snapper," he said. "How's everything going?"

"Okay, under the circumstances," she replied. "Fisher, I want to thank you for the creative way you've been dealing with this crisis."

"That's all right," he said, trying to sound cheerful. "Have you heard much from the other teachers?"

"I've been trying," Ms. Snapper said, with a sigh. "Most of them aren't picking up their phones or responding to e-mails. The few I have touched base with don't sound eager to come back. I don't know what's going on, Fisher. The whole country's gone berserk. I guess we just have to hold on and ride it out."

"Yeah," Fisher said. "I guess so." He wished he could ride it out, but Three's existence was at least partly his fault. The ride wasn't going to stop until he confronted him. "I'll see you later, Ms. Snapper."

He'd left the classroom and closed the door behind him when a breathless boy with dark, disheveled hair ran at him full tilt, barely catching himself before slamming into him.

# Structural Physics of Plant Cell Walls:
## A Marvel of Microscopic Masonry

Period 7 - Lesson plan
* take roll
* recap basic plant cell structure
* skim over plastids/photosynthesis, basic cell function, etc.
* on to our star, microscopic cell walls with great strength, flexibility, and sophistication - review basic function and structure
* next week - get ready for plasmodesma!

KEY POINTS-
* plant cells are unlike animal cells because of the rigid cell wall
* cellulose molecules make up the structural framework of the cells
* hydrogen bonds in cellulose have superb tensile strength, why is this important/awesome?

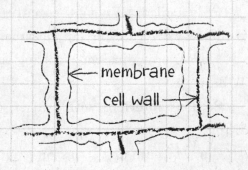

← membrane

cell wall →

"Principal Fisher!" he gasped out, breathless.

"Just call me Fisher," he corrected him patiently. "What's going on?"

"It's gym class," the boy said, running a hand through his hair. "It's . . . I . . . You've . . . Please. Come quick."

The kid tore back down the hall, and Fisher sprinted to keep up.

They careened into the gym, and Fisher skidded to a halt. The Vikings were teaching gym, and Fisher saw instantly that they had invented a new sport. It was a combination of dodgeball, tennis . . . and the piñata.

"Hey!" Fisher shouted, and Willard, Leroy, and Brody paused in the middle of hurling balls at five upside-down kids, whose ankles were secured with climbing ropes. The terrified kids swayed gently back and forth, their faces beet red.

"Well, well," Brody said. "If it isn't the little principal himself."

"What are you doing?" Fisher burst out angrily.

Brody smiled. "What's the matter? You got a problem with how we're running our classroom?"

"We're p-providing the c-cutting edge in phys ed," said Willard.

"So don't interfere with our, er, curry lumber," said Leroy.

"Curr . . . cuh, uh . . . lesson plan," Brody said, trying

124

to correct Leroy, as usual, but unable to remember the word *curriculum*.

Fisher took a deep breath, trying to stay calm. "I appreciate your enthusiasm," he said through gritted teeth, "but target practice isn't education. Take them down and play some real dodgeball. Unless you want to take a turn hanging from the ropes, too?"

"What right do you have to tell us how to teach?" Brody said, hulking toward Fisher. He stopped in front of him and crossed his arms. "What if we say no?"

Fisher drew himself up to his full four feet eleven inches. "Barbecue sauce," he said coldly, staring Brody right in the eyes.

Brody took a quick step back, as though Fisher had punched him. Then he turned around to the other Vikings.

"Fine," he growled. "Willard, Leroy, get 'em down."

"Thank you," said Fisher. The other kids moaned as the Vikings lowered them to the ground and untied their feet. All except Warren Deveraux, who, as usual, had fallen asleep even while upside down. When Brody lowered him to the ground, he popped up like a coiled spring.

"That was great! That was great!" he said. "Are we going to be climbing? Is there a climbing wall? I love to climb!"

Fisher exhaled as he exited the gym. One more crisis averted.

He hadn't taken two steps back into the hallway when two familiar, fuzzy white blurs zipped past him. Alex tore after them.

"Fisher!" he shouted. "Little help?"

Fisher and Alex ran down the hall together as Einy and Berg turned a corner. Fisher and Alex stopped when they made the turn. The hallway was a dead end, but the mice had disappeared.

"Okay," said Fisher. "They must have holed up somewhere. We'll find them." They walked slowly down the hallway, peeking into lockers and poking behind trash cans, squinting under classroom doors and looking in vents.

"What a day," Alex groaned when yet another classroom turned up empty.

"Speaking of that," Fisher said, "have you talked to Amanda today?"

"Not really," said Alex. "She's been . . . not so friendly lately. Like most people."

"I heard," said Fisher. "She's turning her history class into Sparta. She'll probably try to conquer first-period algebra tomorrow."

"Well," Alex said, peering through the vent of an unused locker. "I'll see what I can do. Aha! Got 'em."

Fisher looked through the vent and saw two small white spots sitting on top of a giant heap of bread scraps, pieces of cheese, and vegetables.

"Those tiny criminals," he said. "They must've been stashing stuff here for days. Okay, you open it up and I'll grab them."

"I've got a little cage here," Alex said, putting a shoe box–sized cage on the floor. "Just drop them in and shut it. One, two, three!"

Alex threw the door open, and Fisher grabbed Einy and Berg. They squirmed around in his hands. He was about to drop them into the cage when a barked shout made him spin around.

"So *there* you are!" Amanda yelled. Fisher hadn't heard any footsteps. It was like she'd been hiding in a locker, just waiting to pop out. He reflexively straightened up, trying to give her a smile.

"You're supposed to be running this show," she said, pacing back and forth in front of the Bas boys. "But when I really *need* something, you're just standing around with your hands full of mice."

Fisher quickly dropped Einy and Berg into the cage. By that time, he had little bites on both his thumbs.

"Uh, hi, Amanda . . . ," he said.

"And as if your 'leadership,' or lack of it, wasn't enough cause for concern," she went on, "I'm also dealing with a wombat gone wild. He'll be fine for a while, and then *boom!* He shoots to the window and starts drooling all over the glass like there's somebody blowing a wombat whistle in the front yard. Do you know how hard it is to clean wombat drool off of glass?"

"Look, Amanda," Fisher said, "about your history class . . ."

"Wait, wait," she said, "I know what you're gonna say. And I completely understand. My reenactment of the Battle of Waterloo needs to be full contact. I'll work on that for tomorrow."

"Uh . . . uh . . . ," Fisher stuttered as Amanda spun on her heel and stormed away.

"I . . . don't think she even made eye contact with me," Alex said, looking defeated.

"It's all right," Fisher said. "We'll figure out how this affliction works and we'll cure her. But I'd better go clean these bites," he went on, sighing. "Good luck with the mice."

"Thanks," Alex said. "I think I may just drill some air holes in a safe."

Fisher stopped by the nurse's office. Ben Gomez, an eighth grader with dreams of being a doctor, had enthusiastically taken on the job. He was looking at another student's eye when Fisher came in to wash and bandage his thumbs.

"It's been bothering me since yesterday," the patient said.

"Easy," said Ben as the kid flinched. "You've got a speck

of gravy in there. Trying to pick it out will just push it around and make it worse. Come over to the sink and we'll flush it out."

Fisher straightened up suddenly, as if an electric shock had gone through him. Ben's words rang in his ears. Slowly, a smile spread on his face.

That was it. That was *it*! Three had expected Fisher and Alex to go on the hunt for him. He had orchestrated his whole plan based on that idea.

So Fisher and Alex had to change the game. Maybe, just maybe, they could make Three come to them. They didn't have to find him. They had to *flush him out*.

# ≋ CHAPTER 12 ≋

Welcome to my class. Drop and do twenty push-ups.
No, I'm just kidding. I like to start with a joke.
Drop and do *thirty* push-ups.

—~~Supreme General~~ Glorious Khan Cantrell

"Did you hear everyone talking about the latest *Family Feudalism* episode?" Alex said as they walked home.

"No," Fisher said. "I spent most of the day in the principal's office. And waiting to teach a class that never showed up. And making sure that the Vikings didn't invent a new blood sport."

"Dr. X walked off," said Alex. "After a bomb he put together out of a goat stomach bag and horse manure failed to blow up his brother."

Fisher really didn't want to think about the specific workings of the bomb, so he changed the subject quickly.

"Did you ever get to talk to Amanda?"

"Nope," Alex said. "Didn't even see her leave. I think it's safe to say she's not going to be in a conversing mood anytime soon."

"I think I have an idea of how to deal with Three," Fisher said. "He anticipated our search for him. He manipulated us at every turn. We have to flip the script. We have to make *him* come to *us*."

"That could work," Alex said. They had just reached the Liquid Door. "Can we talk about it over Cheetos? Keeping lunatics in line all day makes me hungry."

"Welcome home, you two!" said Mrs. Bas as soon as Fisher and Alex walked in the front door. "How was school?"

"Uh . . . the usual," Fisher said. "What about you? Good day?"

"Very good," she said, dusting some kind of nutrient powder from her lab gloves. "I got us a new TV for the living room. Why don't you sit down and relax?" Fisher and Alex exchanged a look, wide eyed. Their mom never suggested they watch TV. As if sensing what they were thinking, she laughed. "With all the craziness of the past few days, I think we could all use a little downtime."

"Couldn't agree more," Alex said, flopping onto the couch.

Fisher sat next to him in front of the gleaming new flat screen. "Did Mom really just suggest that we watch TV . . . because it would be good for us?" he said, after Mrs. Bas had gone into the kitchen.

Alex shrugged. "Don't jinx it."

"I hope you two had a marvelous day!" Mrs. Bas said from the kitchen.

Fisher mouthed, *Marvelous?* to Alex. Alex shook his head.

"Maybe she still feels bad about her fight with Dad?" he suggested.

"Maybe . . . ," Fisher said. "But that was days ago." He couldn't shake a weird feeling that his mother was keeping a secret, or trying to hide something.

Alex turned on the TV with a remote control that looked like it could direct space station docking operations. A lot of channels had "technical difficulties" messages up, but plenty were still going.

"There is one conclusion I think we can come to about this whole phenomenon," Alex said, flicking between stations that worked and ones that didn't. "We aren't the only ones unaffected. Ms. Snapper seems normal, and some of the students do, too."

"So maybe the fact that we're unaffected isn't specific to us," Fisher said. "Maybe it's not part of the plan, and we just got lucky somehow, like the other people who are still acting normal."

"I guess it's a question of what we have in common with them," Alex said.

"I think *Family Feudalism* is coming on soon!" came their mom's voice from the kitchen again. "Today's episode has a moat-digging challenge."

A faint squeal followed by a heavy thump announced

FP's arrival downstairs. He trotted into the room, a sweatshirt from the laundry pile he'd crashed in hooked on his ears.

"Hello, boy," Alex said, patting the couch next to him. FP looked up at him for a moment before shaking the shirt loose and jumping up, curling into a little ball next to him. Fisher smiled. At first, the relationship between FP and the clone had been tense at best. With time, they'd begun to get along, especially after FP had gotten over the confusion of having two Fishers when there had once been one.

"I made something for you," Mrs. Bas said, returning to the living room. "Quintuple layer cookies! Chocolate chip and peanut butter cookies sandwiched between marshmallow, with crunchy potato chips on the outside."

The weird feeling Fisher had been fighting since he'd come home began firing off like a rocket. Their mother would never, ever, in a hundred billion years, make them something like that. She wouldn't allow it to come within twenty feet of the house. Alex edged toward Fisher.

"You were right," he whispered. "Something's wrong. She must still be affected. How did she get the oven to cooperate, anyway?"

"Here you go, boys," their mother said, setting the tray of treats on the coffee table. FP stirred from his nap and whined very faintly. As Mrs. Bas pulled her arm away, a drop of something fell from it, hitting the tray and sizzling. It was oil.

And not cooking oil, either. Machine oil.

She started humming as she walked back to the kitchen, and Fisher swore that, underneath the humming, he heard the sounds of tiny servomotors. He felt an army of spiders tiptoeing across his skin, and his pulse started to drum like a runaway jackhammer.

"She's a robot!" whispered Alex and Fisher at the same time.

"So where are our real parents?" Panic was rising up in Fisher's throat.

"We won't know until we deal with her . . . it," Alex corrected himself. Fisher nodded, feeling sick. Alex put a hand on his shoulder and Fisher sucked in a deep breath. He could do this.

"Hey, Mom!" Fisher said in his neediest little-kid voice. "Could we have some water, please?"

"Of course, sweetie," the robot said, in a perfect replication of their mother's voice. "I'll be right in."

Alex slid his hand under the snack tray as the mom-bot walked in with two glasses of water. When mom-bot walked around the couch to the far side of the coffee table and leaned over to set the glasses down, Alex moved. He flipped the tray directly into the robot's face.

As mom-bot recoiled, howling, clawing smashed cookie

from its eyes, Fisher jumped up, seized both glasses from its hands and doused it with water. FP scurried away as sparks showered over the living room.

Alex dove to the floor and wrapped his arms around the robot's legs and Fisher leapt from the couch, vaulted off the coffee table, and put his full weight into the robot's midsection. With Alex holding its legs still, it toppled backward.

"Relax! Relax! Relax!" the robot shrieked in a terrifyingly cheerful tone as it thrashed around on the floor. After Fisher found the access panel behind its neck, opened it, and yanked its control wiring, the robot's hand rocketed out of its arm, punching a hole right through the middle of the new TV.

With the robot disabled, they searched the house to see if their real parents were tied up somewhere. But there was no sign of them. Fisher was just beginning to fear that something unspeakable had happened to them when he turned up a note on the kitchen counter in his father's handwriting, saying they'd gone to try and stock up on nonperishable provisions, since the fridge was still on strike.

Fisher and Alex decided to hide the broken new TV in the best place to camouflage it—under the pile of other TVs that was still in the yard. The mom-bot, they needed to study. Dragging the robot parent up the stairs into Fisher's closet was a challenging task, but cleaning up the trail of cookie crumbs it left in its wake made it almost worth it, especially for FP.

Almost as soon as they'd managed to stuff the mom-bot in Fisher's closet, they heard the front door opening. They hustled the closet closed, left Fisher's room, and headed downstairs.

Their parents walked in wearily, their clothes rumpled, each carrying a pitifully small grocery bag.

"Not a lot of luck," Mr. Bas said. "The place had been looted earlier in the day." Fisher and Alex followed the parents into the kitchen and saw the sorry returns of the expedition: a can of sliced beets, an orange, two boxes of cereal, and a box of frozen chicken wings.

"We'll have to eat these tonight," Mrs. Bas said, holding the wings. "But with no oven or microwave . . ." Everyone's eyes drifted to Lord Burnside, whose own eye spots looked back with what Fisher supposed was a toaster's equivalent of disgust and fear.

"Well," said Lord Burnside, "I—I . . . suppose, if there are no alternatives, I shall do my best to serve. . . ."

"Maybe I can rig up some lab equipment to cook with," said Fisher.

"A very good idea," said Mrs. Bas. "I've been so busy trying to get work done in the middle of this mess that it didn't occur to me. If you could put together a cooking apparatus, I'll get some of that giant rice from the garden."

"Yeah, what have you been working on, Mom?" Fisher asked.

Mrs. Bas began to chop vegetables, "Fisher, you know I cannot disclose my work. Would you mind putting some bread in the coaster? I mean, toaster," she said with a wink.

"I'll go see if I can do something with one of my specimen coolers," said Mr. Bas, giving Mrs. Bas a look.

"I'll help," said Alex.

When the other three had departed, Fisher walked up to the toaster, inspecting Lord Burnside closely. He wondered what his mom meant as he dropped in a slice of sourdough, and gave the toaster a pat.

"Oh, thank you, Master Fisher," Lord Burnside said, relief billowing from him in the form of pleasant-smelling sourdough scents. "You are a just and kind fellow, as I always knew."

"Just trying to do something nice," Fisher said. "You're the only member of our kitchen who's stayed loyal recently, and I think you earned it."

"And ever loyal shall I remain, dear boy," said Lord Burnside. "Thank you again."

# NOTES ON
# MOM-BOT
## by Fisher and Alex

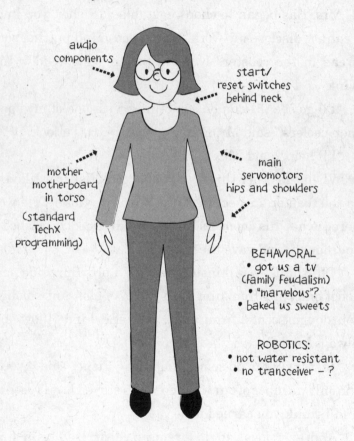

audio components

start/ reset switches behind neck

mother motherboard in torso

(standard TechX programming)

main servomotors hips and shoulders

BEHAVIORAL
• got us a tv (Family Feudalism)
• "marvelous"?
• baked us sweets

ROBOTICS:
• not water resistant
• no transceiver – ?

* * *

After dinner, Fisher and Alex sat in Fisher's room as FP snoozed on the floor, a fleck of buffalo sauce on his lower lip. The mom-bot lay, mostly disassembled, between them. Underneath the incredibly realistic superficial resemblance to Fisher's mom, it was like many of the bots they'd fought in TechX and in LA.

"This is interesting," said Fisher, finishing an exam of its cranium. "There's no transceiver."

"It can't send or receive a radio signal?" Alex said. "That seems . . . primitive."

"Not primitive," Fisher said. "Paranoid. If it's captured, you can't trace it back to its controller. There's no signal to follow."

"And that means," Alex said, looking up at Fisher with excitement glinting in his eyes, "it would have to get its orders and report back in person."

"This is exactly the kind of wild card we need," Fisher said slowly. "I'm not much of a programmer, but I've reset TechX robots before. Three doesn't know that. He can't. With luck, if I can reset this one, its first action will be to report to its controller for orders." He took a deep breath. "Three will walk into *our* trap."

# ≋ CHAPTER 13 ≋

*Only use yourself as bait if you're prepared to be eaten.*
*—Vic Daring, Issue #201*

Alex tiptoed into Fisher's room late that night, wearing all black and carrying an overfull backpack on his shoulder. Fisher was just slipping the last item into his own bag, a tiny pouch of his instant shrub seeds. It was the next step up from the Shrub-in-a-Backpack, allowing his backpack to be used for actually carrying things. FP was walking in excited little circles around Fisher as he packed.

The mom-bot lay on the floor, reassembled, wrapped in a big black bag secured on each side with a rope. The bag was normally used to haul large pieces of lab equipment out into the field. Fisher kept irrationally imagining that the robot would suddenly sit bolt upright, like a vampire awakening in its coffin.

They would take the deactivated robot outside, reset it, and follow it, hopefully to Three's compound. Fisher wished they had a plan for how they would proceed once they got there, but without knowing where Three's base was, how big it was, or what it contained, that was impossible.

Alex looked warily at FP. "What if the pig tries to follow us?"

"I've got something that should do the trick," said Fisher, zipping up a new dark green fleece. "Are you ready?"

"As ready as it's possible to be, I think," said Alex. "I've got a lot of stuff in here. Something's got to work."

"Hope so," Fisher said.

"Okay," said Alex. "I'm going to extend the ladder."

Fisher went and stood by the door as Alex pressed the button to extend the ladder from Fisher's window out over the yard and the wall. The boys had decided it was a useful gadget, even though Alex's existence was no longer a secret.

Fisher raised a thimble-sized object to his ear, meant to enhance his hearing by 175 percent. He listened to make sure that the ladder's muffled squeaks hadn't awoken their parents.

All he heard was a pair of snores, one high and one low, sawing in tandem. That, and Lord Burnside humming English folk tunes to himself.

"It's out," said Alex. "So how about FP? What've you got to keep him out of our hair?"

Fisher opened his closet door. Inside was a wheeled contraption, which he pulled into the middle of the room. It was assembled around his old popcorn gun. The original had been lost during his infiltration of TechX, but this new model was polished and ready to go.

FP's ears began twitching excitedly.

The new and improved popcorn gun was set into a rolling frame that pointed it straight up in the air. A metal coil wrapped around its trigger and was connected to a series of gears and cogs, and on the outside of the frame was a simple analog timer dial. Fisher turned the dial to its maximum setting.

With creaks and pops, the gears started to turn. After fifteen seconds, the machine's coil briefly tightened around the trigger and a few pieces of popcorn spat from the gun, falling to the floor. FP's eyes locked on to them and he dove like a hawk onto the nearest kernel. He munched for a few seconds, looking happily up at Fisher, before trotting to the next.

"This will spit out a few kernels every fifteen seconds for at least a couple of hours," Fisher said. "It'll keep him occupied."

A few more kernels popped, and FP leap-glided to try and catch them, opening his mouth in anticipation. The kernels bounced squarely off his snout, and FP tumbled to the ground and rolled a somersault. He scrunched up his eyes and shook his head in surprise, sniffling as the kernels fell around him. He grabbed them up from the floor and awaited the next round.

# Schematics for Reconfigured
# POPCORN GUN

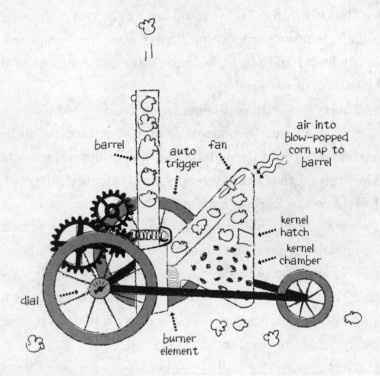

With FP staring at the popcorn gun machine as if it were a sorcerous fountain pouring forth the elixir of eternal life, Fisher led the way down and across the ladder, holding the mom-bot by one end. Alex took the other end and gently lowered it out the window. It was heavy, and after only a few minutes, Fisher's arms were shaking. They stopped frequently to catch their breaths as they passed slowly over the garden, toward the wall that divided the Bas property from the street.

The only things Fisher could hear as he inched his way along the downward-sloping ladder were the faint creak of the metal and plastic beneath him, and Alex's careful breathing just behind him.

There was only one benefit, as far as he could see, to the crazy pox. Ordinarily, Fisher and Alex had to be extremely careful traveling along the ladder so as not to alert any of the security robots that patrolled the yard. But since the kitchen appliances had started acting up, Fisher's parents had disabled almost all of their robotic equipment. Even if the times were getting more dangerous, it was better to have no security against burglars than a security system that had already broken down your door and stuck you to the wall with instant plaster by the time the burglars arrived.

They reached the end of the ladder at last, and Fisher crouched on top of the wall, looking down the street one way and then the other.

"Okay," he whispered back. "We're clear. Now push!"

Alex pushed as Fisher pulled, and together they shoved the mom-bot over the wall. It landed on the sidewalk below, its impact muffled by the thick, padded bag. Fisher dropped next to it, and Alex landed softly a moment later.

They unzipped the bag and hauled the robot to its feet.

"Here goes," said Fisher, toggling a pair of switches behind its neck. Both boys backed quickly away, prepared to spring at it if they had to.

Its eyes opened to the faint whirr of motors. Now that Fisher knew it was a robot, he couldn't believe he'd ever mistaken it for his real mom.

The robot looked ahead, left, and right, without registering either Alex or Fisher. Then it made a few small clicks with its tongue, said, "Control," and started walking.

Fisher and Alex nodded to each other excitedly, and they crept after it.

It was heading away from Wompalog and downtown, which surprised Fisher. There wasn't anything but houses in that direction for several miles. Maybe Three had taken over somebody's home? Or maybe he had an accomplice?

After three blocks, the robot took such an abrupt turn that Fisher had to leap back to avoid crashing into it. It headed across the still-empty street at a trot, straight for a small park that was ringed by thick trees.

"This can't be right," whispered Alex. "How could Three hide such a sophisticated operation in a neighborhood park?"

"Only one way to find out," said Fisher. "Let's hang back and see where it goes."

The mom-bot continued into the park, and Fisher and Alex ducked into the trees, concealing themselves behind leafy branches. A few street lamps stood among the trees.

Fisher could make out a little conical shape right in the middle of the baseball diamond.

As his eyes adjusted to the dark, he realized it was a tent.

"Is that a tent?" Alex whispered, echoing his thoughts.

"Looks like one," Fisher said. "Maybe camouflaging the entrance to an underground base?"

The mom-bot, now merely a fuzzy shadow in the darkness, stopped directly in front of the tent. The flap opened, and another shadowy figure emerged.

Fisher tensed.

"Stun sticks," he said. "Let's see if we can close in on him before he knows we're here."

Fisher crept left. Alex went right. Fisher thought he could hear faint words exchanged between the mom-bot and the figure he assumed was Three, but the sound was drowned out by his own cymbal-crash heartbeat. The stun stick quivered in his grip as he inched forward.

Then the shadowy figure suddenly struck out, and the mom-bot collapsed. There was a loud click, a bright light came on, and Fisher was blinded.

*A trap!* he thought. *It was another trap!*

He stumbled back, trying to regain the cover of the trees, when a voice came out of the blinding light.

"Oh, good. I was hoping she would work to draw you out. How nice to see you again."

Fisher's blood froze in his veins. It wasn't Three's voice. He blinked furiously to clear his vision. The light dimmed slightly, and an all-too familiar figure stood before them: a slightly built man, with thin black hair slicked straight back and a hooked nose that gave his already angular face the cruel, powerful menace of a bird of prey.

"Granger," growled Fisher.

"Hello, Fisher," said Dr. X. "You look as though you weren't expecting—?"

Before he could say any more, Alex's stun stick whistled through the air and cracked Granger on the head. Granger staggered back. A second and a half later, Alex's fist found the same spot, and the man Fisher used to know as Harold Granger collapsed onto the grass.

By the time Fisher reached Granger's side, Alex had pulled him to his feet and twisted one arm behind his back. Fisher was impressed by Alex's combat skills. Maybe Amanda had been giving him lessons.

"Wait!" Dr. X said, a thin red trickle flowing down his forehead, wincing as Alex gave his arm a push. "Don't kill me until you hear what I've got to say."

"Unlike *you*," Alex said, punctuating the *you* with another push to the twisted arm, "I don't kill unarmed people for kicks. I will, however, make sure the police have a hard time identifying your face underneath all the bruises when they come to arrest you."

"Tell us where Three is," Fisher said, holding the buzzing stun stick inches from Dr. X's hawk nose. "How long have you been working with him? Where does the tent lead? What kind of secret lab have you been building?"

"It's just a tent," Dr. X said piteously. "It leads to the inside of a tent. No secret labs. No labs at all! I'm not working with Three. And please—ow—before you throw me to the law, you need to listen to what I have to say."

"So start *talk*ing," said Alex, tightening his hold.

"I'm—agh—not here to fight you. In fact, I'm here to help you."

"Help us?" squawked Fisher. "Have you forgotten that the last time we saw you, you tried to tear us to pieces with an army of metal henchmen?"

"Not at all," said Dr. X. His grimace of pain turned briefly into a smile. "But this is the difference between what people like you call good guys and bad guys. Good guys have principles and rules.

"We bad guys, on the other hand, work for ourselves and for our own personal gains. We will work with whomever it is in our best interest to work with at any given moment. It doesn't matter that I was gleefully anticipating your destruction weeks ago. In my current situation, you can help me. And I believe I can help you. So for the moment, I'm over it."

"Over it?" Fisher repeated. "You mean over your desire to kill us?"

Dr. X inclined his head in a nod.

"Sorry if that doesn't make us want to trust you," growled Alex. It was clearly taking all of his willpower to keep from pummeling Dr. X into the ground until the pummeling set off the San Andreas Fault. Alex was obviously *not* over the fact that Dr. X had very nearly killed him.

"I'm not asking you to trust me," said Dr. X. "I'm simply asking you to—ow!—work with me. You are scientists. Consider this situation rationally. I have been deposed by Three. I have no resources available to me, other than my admittedly gigantic intellect. Three is in command of everything I once owned. He knows that we are the biggest possible threats to him. Therefore, we are all his targets. And the only reasonable way to fight against the power he commands is to combine our efforts."

The stun stick was shaking in Fisher's hand. Mr. Granger had been a trusted teacher and friend once. Then he had kidnapped Alex to force Fisher's mother to betray her colleagues and the government, and hand over the AGH to him. He revealed himself to be Dr. X in the process. Fisher and Alex had almost gotten vaporized in their escape from his compound. When they'd thought Dr. X was finally gone, he'd reemerged and tried to end their lives all over again. And now, here he was, if not asking for their friendship, then at least claiming to be on their side.

"We have no way of knowing he's not still working with Three," Alex said to Fisher. "This whole deposed routine might just be an act."

"Boys, if I wanted to fool you, I could do it in a hundred different ways, as I demonstrated in LA."

Dr. X had a very good point. But Fisher wasn't ready to relent. Dr. X had tried to wipe out him and Alex more than once—and he'd threatened their mother and father to boot.

"So what about the robot?" he said. "If you're not working with Three, how'd you engineer it?"

"I didn't," Dr. X said, still wincing in Alex's grip. "I merely reprogrammed it, as you did. Remember, I pioneered the technology that all of Three's robots are based on. I understand how they work. I've been keeping watch on you for days. I recognized the robot for what it was immediately. Impressive modification, I must admit. Three applied his own genetic material to the robot's silicon surface so that your Liquid Door would let it pass. I anticipated that you would discover it was a fake, and programmed it to return here if reactivated, hoping you'd follow."

"I'm guessing you reprogrammed its mission, too, so it wouldn't kill us," said Alex.

"No," Dr. X conceded. "The only thing I altered was its home base location. I don't know what its original mission was, nor did I try to change it."

Fisher and Alex frowned at each other.

"That doesn't make any sense," Fisher said. "All it did was give us cookies."

"And try and get us to watch TV," Alex added.

A small trill of excitement zipped up Fisher's spine. "TV . . . ," he said, recalling the mom-bot's insistence that they turn on *Family Feudalism*. "Wait a minute. What if getting us to watch TV *was* the robot's mission?"

Alex finally let go of Dr. X's arm. Dr. X tried to massage some feeling back into his shoulder.

"What if the crazy pox isn't biological *or* chemical?" Fisher said excitedly. "What if it's a *transmission*?"

"A radio or television broadcast could have a subliminal element," Dr. X said. "Over time, it might affect behavior."

"It would have to be something popular," said Alex. "To engineer behavioral changes this significant, it would have to have a cumulative effect and build up over time. Rewire the mind bit by bit."

Fisher nodded.

"Okay. So people would have to be exposed to it regularly over a long period of time. Like a new fad show that everyone's watching and talking . . ." Alex stopped. *"Family Feudalism.* Which is what the mom-bot was trying to make us watch."

Fisher frowned. "The crazy pox started soon after the show went on the air. We'd watched six episodes before the fall formal, and that night we almost knocked each other's teeth out. We and our parents were affected until Dad threw the TVs away. Veronica was affected until she was grounded and couldn't watch TV anymore."

"And Ms. Snapper was affected until she accidentally destroyed her TV," Fisher continued. "CURTIS watches TV all the time. And most of our kitchen appliances are designed to receive broadcast signals, too. But Lord Burnside isn't."

"All the evidence points to it," Alex said.

"It's ingenious, really," said Dr. X. "I wish I'd thought of it."

Fisher turned to him. "You've provided us with valuable intelligence," he said, although he hated to admit it. "Is there any other way you can be useful to us?"

"Oh, yes," said Dr. X. "Have a look at this." He backed up to the tent. Fisher and Alex drew their stun guns.

"Don't try anything funny," Fisher warned.

Slowly, keeping his eyes on Fisher and Alex, Dr. X knelt and rummaged around with one hand inside the tent. He extracted a thick stick somewhat taller than he was and straightened up again.

"A stick," said Alex dully.

"Not 'a stick,'" said Dr. X. "An English quarterstaff. It is an old and venerable martial art that I had the privilege to study while on the set of *Family Feudalism*. I actually got quite good at it. You'll need all the fighting help you can get, soon enough."

Fisher and Alex looked at each other. After a moment, Alex nodded, very slightly.

Fisher looked back at Dr. X. "I don't trust you, and I don't like you. But you're right about one thing. We need all the help we can get right now. Will you work with us to bring Three down?"

"My boy," Fisher's former biology teacher said, raising the staff to his heart and smiling, "it would be an absolute pleasure."

## ≋ CHAPTER 14 ≋

This is it, the final battle we have to fight.

Unless there's a Four out there somewhere.

If there's a Four, I'm just going to retire. Probably to Saturn.

—Fisher Bas, Personal Notes

"Ho! Ha!" Dr. X shouted as he demonstrated his skill with the staff. "Guard! Turn! Parry! Dodge! Spin! Thrust!"

"All right," Fisher said, "I believe you. Let's focus, okay? Can you recover the robot's original home location?"

"I don't know," said Dr. X. "But I'll take a stab at it."

"Well, get cracking," said Alex. "In the meantime, we'll . . ." He trailed off, cocking his head to the side. "Does anybody else hear that?"

"Sounds like an . . ." But Fisher didn't get the chance to say "earthquake." What started as a low hum grew slowly, steadily, and transformed into a rhythm. He looked down and saw dust and pebbles hopping from the vibration. But it was too regular to be an earthquake. It sounded almost like . . . footsteps.

Thousands and thousands of footsteps.

Fisher, Alex, and Dr. X dashed to the edge of the park.

Fisher felt like the world had been kicked out from under him.

Figures were marching in the streets. In the faint moonlight, he couldn't tell who or what they were. But there were hundreds of them. Maybe thousands.

An army.

And in the air, dozens of tiny objects, visible from their faint blinking red lights, were spiraling. They were coming down all over the town. One landed on the corner of the next street.

"Come on," Fisher said.

They reached the small device just as its top unfolded into a complex series of lenses. After a few seconds, it projected a life-sized hologram.

"Three," breathed Alex, Fisher, and Dr. X at the same time.

Three was projected in front of them, dressed in a dark gray suit cut and tailored like a military uniform, with an officer's cap pulled low to hide his eyes. His face was barely lit, as in Dr. X's old videos, so it would not be recognizable.

"Good morning, citizens of Palo Alto," the clone began, his voice charged with a passionless but piercing electricity. "I am sure many of you are confused and afraid about what is happening in your city, and indeed in the wider world. I'm afraid I must confirm your fears: There is chaos in the streets. Crime is everywhere. It is unsafe to travel, and conflict is threatening to tear our communities apart. I'm afraid this is only the beginning of a long, dark era. I bring you good news, however. I have foreseen these events, and have been preparing for them for some time. Even now my loyal servants are moving into place, dedicated to protecting order and, more importantly, protecting you. Together we can ride out the storm.

"That is all for now," Three said, his silhouetted face inclining in a nod. "I will address you all again soon."

The hologram blinked off. After a short delay, it blinked back on and the message repeated.

"So now we know what he's been planning all this time," Alex said grimly.

"And why he sent us on our wild goose chase," Fisher said. "He was keeping us busy so he'd have time to build this army. By morning, when most people see this message, his soldiers will be everywhere. What do you want to bet they'll come for us soon?"

"We have to go for him first," said Alex. He sucked in a deep breath. "We need Amanda," he blurted out. "We need everyone we can get."

"But can we convince her to help us when she's still affected? I'm not getting rid of Three just to see him replaced by Undying Chancellor Times Infinity Cantrell or whatever title she decided on. "

"Maybe we can cut power to her house," suggested Alex. "Give her until tomorrow to get over the effects of the brainwashing broadcast."

"Do you really think that one of your twelve-year-old peers is going to be of any use to us?" Dr. X said to Fisher with a smirk. "I taught at Wompalog, remember. I can't recall being impressed by anyone's potential to defeat the most calculating and powerful villain of our time."

"You'll remember this one," Fisher said. "The last time you saw her, she was tearing your robot army apart."

"Ah," said Dr. X as the smile faded from his face. "Well, if you want to disable her home's electricity, I can repro-gram the robot to do just that," he concluded.

"All right," Fisher said. "Let's get it back home before Three takes over the streets."

Alex and Fisher retrieved the mom-bot from the park and hefted it into the air. Dr. X trailed behind them, quarterstaff in hand. Dim shadows were assembling a few blocks away from the park, but the street leading back toward the Bas home was still clear.

The mom-bot's weight dug into Fisher's right shoul-der as he ran, thumping his collarbone with each step. Shadows flickered in the corner of his vision. Were they Three's henchmen, waiting to spring?

"Keep up the pace!" Alex half whispered.

Fisher heard footsteps about a block away. Quick ones.

Were those just their footsteps echoing off the houses? He couldn't quite be sure.

The house was in sight, and Dr. X's breathing was getting louder and harsher. The sprint was clearly not his event. Fisher's breathing pounded in his ears as they rounded a corner, and the wall around the Bas house became visible.

"Front gate!" Alex said. "Front gate!" It would take time to pull the mom-bot back up the wall. They'd have to risk going in the front way, even if the noise might disturb their parents.

Alex and Fisher skidded to a halt at the Liquid Door front gate, which turned from a suspended near solid to a cloud in their presence. They stayed in place so that Dr. X, whom the gate wouldn't recognize, could pass through as well.

Only after they were through the gate and had set down the mom-bot did Fisher breathe a faint, relieved sigh. His shoulders were aching and he felt a throb in arm muscles he never knew even existed.

"Okay," he whispered to Dr. X. "Let's get to work reprogramming this thing."

"Out here?" Dr. X frowned.

"My parents are asleep," he answered sharply. "I don't want my mom coming face-to-face with her own imposter—or with you. Once we've set the robot on its way, we'll

# Schematics for
# LIQUID GATE

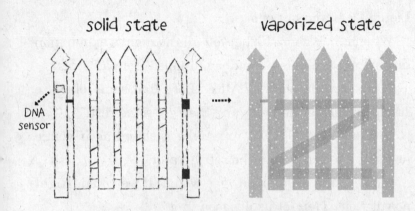

solid state       vaporized state

DNA sensor

go inside and find you a place to hide."

The three set to work, guided by the dim beam of Fisher's flashlight, which he fished out of his backpack. Dr. X fiddled away, making occasional noises of disgust or satisfaction. If their plan worked, the robot would proceed to Amanda's house, cut the power, transmit a "mission success" message and then self-destruct.

"All right," said Dr. X, after nearly an hour "Stand back."

Fisher and Alex took a few steps backward as Dr. X threw the mom-bot's power switch and backpedaled, holding his staff at the ready.

The mom-bot twitched a few times, made a few garbled digital noises, and sat up. It rotated its head back and forth, stood, and turned to Dr. X.

"Orders confirmed," it said, and it slipped through the Liquid Door and out of sight.

When it had gone, Fisher felt all the night's exhaustion hit him at once, like a sandbag dropped from a ladder.

"Come on," he said to Alex. "Let's find some place to stash our former nemesis and then get some rest."

*"Stash?"* said Dr. X. "You make it sound as if you're just going to toss me in the refrigerator."

"Believe me," Alex said, "we would, if we could. Right now it won't even let us put food in it."

As Fisher snuck through the front door, he was hit with a powerful urge to pull Alex in with him and slam the door, locking Dr. X outside. Dr. X had caused both of them terrible suffering and there was no reason to believe he wouldn't do it again given the chance.

But the fresh memory of Three's mysterious army moving into position was enough to stifle his impulse. Working with Dr. X really was the only way to stop Three. But Fisher swore to himself that once Three was out of the way, he would finally see Dr. X brought to justice.

# CHAPTER 15

*Fool! Do you know who I am?*
*Do you know what I've done??*
*Do you know what this device I have is?! . . .*
*Seriously, do you know what this is? I just found it.*


—Prince Xultar of Venus, enemy of Vic Daring, Issue #30


Ms. Snapper sent word out early the next morning that Wompalog had officially been closed down for the foreseeable future. As she was the only teacher still sane, the news was unsurprising, to say the least.

Fisher and Alex picked over their breakfast of leftover chicken wings, occasionally glancing up at their parents. Mr. and Mrs. Bas were reading the one newspaper in the city still in circulation, the *Daily Harbinger*, the local sensationalist tabloid. Most of its stories involved alien abduction, Elvis sightings, or abduction by aliens dressed as Elvis.

"Apparently, a recent construction project disturbed the underground lair of a five-thousand-year-old cult of witch turtles," Mrs. Bas said, folding the paper over a picture of a snapping turtle with a pointy black hat crudely Photoshopped onto its head.

"Maybe they were underground to escape the talking lobsters . . . from space," said Mr. Bas, scrutinizing another article.

They both sighed. Mr. Bas looked across the table at Fisher and Alex.

"Your mother and I are attempting to work out what's causing this mass chaos," he said. "We're in contact with a few colleagues of ours who haven't succumbed to it . . ." He drifted off and looked at Fisher's mom, a lightbulb going off above his head. "Instead of us looking out to space, perhaps there is a way to bring the Unknown Universe to us."

"Yes, dear. Something to ponder on, certainly. Fisher, it's hard to say how long it'll take us to find a solution," Mrs. Bas added. "But we're going to keep plugging away until we do. If you need anything, we'll be in our labs. Just be careful, and stay inside, okay?"

Fisher wondered if Alex felt the same guilty pinprick in the stomach that he did. He ducked his head and triple-checked the message he'd received early that morning— the mom-bot had succeeded in cutting Amanda's power. By now the fiendish android was a puddle of melted alloy and plastic, an image he didn't dwell on.

The brothers wolfed down the rest of their breakfasts, checked to make sure their parents were both upstairs, grabbed some equipment, and headed down to the basement.

The basement of the Bas house was not the beeping, clicking technological wonder that most people assumed it was. The Bases didn't have their own nuclear reactor down there, or a hidden city of automated servants that worked to keep the house's machinery going. Mr. Bas's bio lab had been in the basement, but after the AGH project had been canceled, Mrs. Bas had needed storage space for all the equipment she was no longer using, and he'd consolidated to his smaller lab on the second floor.

So now their basement was just a vast space full of stuff that was either useless or, in rare cases, had never been used in the first place. Cases and cases of test tubes, beakers, and flasks on top of storage units and crates full of air hoses and microscope lens cases. Mr. Bas's first astronomical telescope sat in one corner, pointed up at the cement ceiling in futility. There were also storage shelves for new equipment and parts that the Bases didn't need yet, or simply didn't have space for upstairs.

More mundane objects were mixed in with the clutter as well. There was a framed picture of Mr. Bas standing next to a colony of muddy waterfowl. The bicycle that Fisher had ridden three times before he'd flipped over the handlebars into a pond full of unfriendly turtles and swore never to ride again. The washer and dryer that Fisher's parents had let him use once when he was eight, when he'd used the tumble dryer to conduct an experiment studying the effects of gravel erosion on cotton—specifically, all of his parents' socks.

Fisher and Alex waded through the experimental debris until they reached a door that led to a sectioned-off portion of the basement—a door neither of their parents had passed through for at least three years. Fisher had secured it with a padlock, just in case. He pulled out a key from the chain he was wearing around his neck.

He pushed open the creaky door to reveal a small, dusty room lit with unflattering fluorescent lights, which shone down on old, collapsing weight benches, rusted dumbbells, and a lonely stationary bike, whose pedals had fallen off and sat on the floor like the dried-up fruit of a dead tree.

This was the workout room that their parents had put together when they'd first moved in. Since that initial day, it had probably been used only once or twice.

Sitting on the floor, next to a rusted barbell, was Dr. X. He sat cross-legged, his hands resting in his lap, palms turned up.

"What are you doing?" said Alex as Fisher closed and locked the door behind them. He set down his backpack and removed his laptop, opening it and sitting cross-legged on the floor.

"I was meditating," said Dr. X.

"Meditating?" repeated Fisher.

"When one has an immense catalogue of knowledge in one's mind as I do, and such feverish powers of calculation, it is occasionally necessary to clear the head, let the brain cool off a bit."

"Your plan worked," said Fisher, ignoring Dr. X's immense egotism. "If we can get past Three's henchmen in the street, Amanda should be willing to help us. But where do we go from there? We don't have any leads."

"Actually," Dr. X said, standing up and stretching his back, "we do. When we reprogrammed the android, I was able to download the contents of its memory onto my personal portable computing and communications terminal."

"Your smart phone," Alex said, raising his eyebrows.

*"Anyway,"* Dr. X continued, frowning at Alex, "I spent much of the night sifting through this data and discovered its report-in location."

"And?" Fisher said.

"Funny, really," Dr. X said. "It's the very place I used to teach you biology."

"Wompalog??" Alex said. "Three's made his home base *our school*?"

"Not necessarily," Dr. X said. "It could simply be a designated meeting spot for his agents. But even if he isn't there, it's likely we can find clues there that will help us locate him."

There was a pinging sound. It was Fisher's phone,

alerting him that he had a new e-mail. He opened it nervously. It was a school-wide message, sent from another Wompalog seventh grader.

"Hang on . . . ," he said as he opened it up. It was a link to a video that had already received over a million views. Alex and Dr. X moved behind him to watch.

It began with sad violin music playing over scenes of vandalism, looting, and traffic jams devolving into fistfights. The scenes faded out as Three came into view, wearing the same uniform and low-pulled cap as he'd been wearing in the holographic message. He was standing in a plain-looking room of gray-painted concrete. Behind him were a few wires and exposed pipes, dangling from one section of the cracked ceiling.

"Ladies and gentlemen," Three began, "you have already observed my task force of mechanical, remotely operable, semi-intelligent drones. They are humanlike robots, or androids."

The video cut to a new image, and Fisher and Alex nearly leapt out of their shoes.

The image was a column, ten wide and eight deep, of androids.

Androids that looked exactly like Fisher and Alex.

All of them were wearing the same sort of gray uniform Three was, but without the cap.

"My androids have been deployed throughout the city,"

Three went on. "They will now be assuming peacekeeping operations. All traffic and transportation will be logged, checked, and monitored . . . for your safety. They will deal with civil unrest and incidents of crime, in whatever way they deem necessary. Soon peace will be restored. My androids are here to help you, and I urge you to fully cooperate with them.

"I urge you *strongly*."

The video faded out.

Dr. X's eyes had misted over a bit. "He is truly my greatest creation ever. . . ." He sighed. "A little *too* great."

Fisher pocketed his phone and sat down. The end of the world was here, and it literally wore his face.

"We have no time to waste," Alex said, his voice shaking slightly. "Even getting to school is going to be tough with the . . . Three-bots around. By now they've probably set up checkpoints and guard posts. Not to mention patrols."

"Three has assembled massive power," said Dr. X. "Wherever he is, getting inside may well be impossible."

"With all due respect, Dr. X," Fisher said, managing a wry smile, "I've heard that before."

Dr. X opened his mouth to reply but found no good words in grasping distance.

"Let's start gearing up," Alex said. "We can get Amanda on the way."

"We should get Wally, too," said Fisher. "If ever there was a time to lure Mason out, it's now."

Alex shook his head. "I worry that wherever he is, Mason isn't coming back," he said darkly.

"But we have to try," Fisher insisted. Making a sudden decision, he said, "FP will come, too. He proved invaluable when we infiltrated TechX."

Dr. X frowned.

Fisher and Alex took Dr. X to the front yard and locked him in one of their mom's gardening sheds. They were keeping him away from technology at all costs. He could do damage with a rake and a watering can, true, but nothing compared to what he might do if he accessed any of the Bases' laboratory equipment. And though he was an ally—temporarily—neither of the boys trusted him.

The boys went upstairs to retrieve a selection of the gear they had taken with them the night before. This time, they selected only the most important items, so they would not be weighed down.

Alex packed a water bottle full of his Instant Ice. So long as it stayed sealed in the bottle, it would remain in a liquid state. When poured, thrown, or flung from the bottle, it would solidify almost instantly. He also packed a small bag of Spider Marbles. The little spheres would roll freely while clinging to any surface, including walls and ceilings.

Some were fitted with cameras; others, small hooks.

Fisher had been served well by his elastic necktie in the past, and he tested its strength quickly before packing it. Then he held up his electric stun stick, thumbing the button and letting it crackle for a moment.

They'd made Alex a spy suit, and upgraded Fisher's to be sleeker and better fitting, with improved climbing grips on the soles and gloves. A small pouch on each suit's back contained a piece of technology the brothers had developed together. Although Shrub-in-a-Backpack was effective, Alex realized to go up against Three, he needed something with a little more teeth. So he had created the Thornbush-in-a-Pouch.

"Do you have our special weapon?" Fisher asked as Alex came into his room, still double-checking his gear.

"It's stowed safely," Alex said, patting his bag. "I just hope it works the way it did in beta testing."

FP was hopping around in his own mini–spy suit as Fisher finished organizing his things. There wasn't a single popcorn kernel, not even a trace of one, anywhere in Fisher's room. Fisher looked over the elaborate machine he had set up the night before to distract FP, shrugged, and dismounted the popcorn gun from it.

"Could come in handy," he said, slinging it over his back. "Are you ready, boy? Ready to put a stop to yet another world-threatening maniac?"

# THORNBUSH-IN-A-POUCH
## (PATENT PENDING)

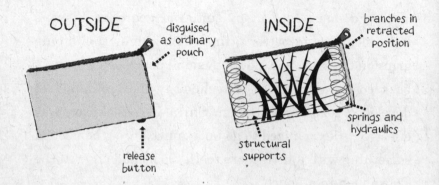

OUTSIDE

disguised as ordinary pouch

release button

INSIDE

branches in retracted position

springs and hydraulics

structural supports

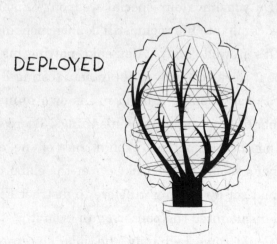

DEPLOYED

FP shook his head around, his ears flapping as they tried to keep up, then looked up at Fisher with an excited grin.

"All right, then," he said. "Here we go."

The robot army had begun marching at midnight. It was now late afternoon the next day, and all was quiet. That meant only one thing: Three's servants were all finally in place.

Fisher, Alex, and FP went quietly downstairs and out to the front yard. They unlocked the gardening shed and gestured Dr. X out from its depths.

"Ready?" said Fisher.

"Ready," said Alex.

"Ready," said Dr. X. "Do you have a plan to reach Amanda's house?"

"Alex," Fisher said, "you remember that abandoned pizza delivery car we saw parked down the block?"

"Yes . . . why?" Alex said.

"The keys were sitting on the driver's seat," Fisher said.

"I don't like where this is going . . . ," said Dr. X.

"I suggest you start liking it," Fisher said. "You're driving."

Alex poked his head through the front gate—literally—then waved Fisher and Dr. X through it. FP stayed close on Fisher's heels. He seemed to realize serious business was happening. His eyes darted back and forth, and he kept his snout to the ground.

They were in luck. There weren't any guards posted on their street—at least, not yet. They kept their heads down and walked quickly to where the delivery vehicle was, thankfully, still parked, doors ajar, down the block.

"I should warn you," Dr. X said as he climbed into the driver's seat, "I haven't driven an automobile voluntarily in some years."

"If makes you feel better, you're not driving an automobile *voluntarily* now, either," growled Alex as he got into the front passenger seat. Fisher got in the backseat behind him, and put the middle seat belt around FP as best he could.

"Okay," Fisher said. "Go slowly at first. We need to get past the . . . Fisher-bots without arousing their suspicion."

"Fisher-bots?" said Alex, turning to look back at him as Dr. X turned the ignition. The car lurched away from the curb.

Fisher shook his head. "Their existence is as much my fault as Three's," he said. "I'm only being honest about it."

The car moved slowly and jerkily down the street, and Fisher held on, sliding as low in the seat as he could manage. Every lurch made him hold on tighter. He tried to keep one hand on FP to keep the little pig from bouncing around.

"Left here," said Alex, and the car turned like a sleep-deprived hippo. "Fisher-bots ahead," he said, immediately after Dr. X made the turn. He slouched down in his seat. "Act like a pizza, Fisher."

Fisher flattened himself onto the backseat, keeping FP shielded beneath him. Seconds passed, and Dr. X rolled the car forward.

"We're in the clear," Dr. X said finally.

Fisher sat up, exhaling. They were almost at Amanda's street.

"Keep straight," Alex said.

Dr. X's fingers tightened on the wheel. "Bad news. There's a checkpoint at the next intersection," he said. "Should I stop or crash through it?"

Fisher craned his neck so he could scope out the checkpoint. Two bots stood next to a police line–style wooden roadblock.

"I vote crash," Alex said. "Fisher?"

"I have another idea," he said. "Pull over."

A minute later, the Fisher-bots watched what looked like a walking pizza box approach their checkpoint. Fisher's entire head and torso were dwarfed behind the enormous lid, which was open, like a mouth.

*"Hey, you two!"* Fisher said in a cartoony, high voice.

*"Who wants some pizza? Fresh baked several days ago! Two toppings, and it talks! What more could you ask for??"*

The bots stepped forward to examine the talking pizza.

There was a loud *crack*, and then a blur of motion. One of the bots fell over, its head dented in. The other bot whipped around to face Dr. X, who stood crouched in a fighting stance, his staff at the ready.

"An army of Fishers was *my* idea," he said in an icy voice. "And I hate copycats."

The bot rushed him, but a second solid *thwack* put it out of commission.

"You really are handy with that," said Alex.

Dr. X bowed.

"We're almost there," Fisher said. "Let's go!"

They piled back in the car. Dr. X reversed, swerved around the wooden roadblock . . . and then crashed straight into a lamppost, killing the engine.

"I warned you," said Dr. X as he got out of the car. He looked at the steam pouring out of the hood.

"Now we'll have to get to Wompalog on foot," said Alex.

"We're losing time," said Fisher, with growing frustration. Luckily, they were only a few houses down from Amanda's. He turned to Alex. "Stay here with him"— he gestured to Dr. X—"until I call for you. I better warn Amanda that Dr. X is with us. Otherwise she'll have him in a headlock before I get the chance to explain."

FP trotted after Fisher as Fisher jogged to Amanda's house and knocked on the door. He needed an excuse in case her mom or dad answered the door.

But to his surprise, Amanda herself opened the door.

"Fisher?" She scowled. "What are you doing here?"

Wally peeked out from behind her legs. When he saw FP, the two darted out into the yard and started to chase each other in circles.

"Look, you know how everyone's been acting . . . weird lately?" Fisher said. Amanda nodded, watching him suspiciously. "It's all Three's fault. And we need your help to stop him."

Amanda exhaled slowly. "I knew it," she said. "At last, I knew you, or one of the other . . . yous . . . had to be tangled up in this." She sighed. "Is there a plan?"

"Yes," said Fisher. "And we've picked up an . . . unlikely ally." He took a deep breath. Now came the hard part. "Listen, I need you to trust me and Alex."

"What are you talking about?" Amanda said.

"I'm talking about . . . Dr. X," said Fisher. "We're working with him. Or he's working with us."

"*What??*" Amanda said. Her eyes bugged out so far, they practically dislodged her glasses. "Are you *insane*??"

"Probably," admitted Fisher. "But we haven't got a choice. Promise me you won't demolish him on sight."

Amanda looked away. A muscle worked in her jaw. "I . . . promise," she muttered at last. Then she turned back to him. "So are we going to do this or not?"

Fisher nodded. "Where are your parents? Do you have to leave them a note or something?"

Amanda waved a hand. "They're in the basement playing Monopoly," she said. "Have been ever since we lost power last night. They won't even notice I'm gone."

Fisher signaled to Alex, who was still waiting down the street with Dr. X, half concealed behind the still-smoking car. Alex gripped Dr. X by the arm and marched him over to Amanda's house.

"You," Amanda said, eyes blazing. She cocked back her right arm. Fisher stepped in between them.

"No," he said. "You promised."

She kept her fist where it was—directly in line with Dr. X's nose.

"Amanda," Alex cut in, "we have to stop Three. Millions of people could be hurt by him if we don't. And we need all the help we can get." His voice dropped to a whisper. "I promise . . . when we're done, I won't stop you. Heck, I'll sell tickets and popcorn." He smiled a little.

Amanda grumbled something and dropped her hand.

Just then there were footsteps in the dark hallway beyond her.

And Veronica Greenwich stepped out onto the porch next to her.

"Veronica?!" Fisher said. He feared for a second the crazy pox actually had affected him, and he was seeing things.

"Hey, Fisher," said Veronica quietly. Her face was pale and her eyes were ringed with dark circles. "I was visiting Amanda, trying to smooth things out when her power went out. My parents thought it'd be safer if I stayed put." She took a deep breath. "Funny you're here. I was hoping you might be able to explain some things. Such as exactly what's happening. And why there are a thousand androids with your face imposing martial law on Palo Alto."

Fisher met Veronica's gaze. He realized that she had every right not to trust him. He'd been lying to her from the beginning. It was a bad habit, and he figured he had more than enough of those already.

"I . . . I haven't been totally honest with you," he said, his heart thudding into his ribs. "But I'm going to fix that." He took a deep breath. "Alex isn't my cousin." Veronica looked from him to Alex. When she saw Dr. X, whom she recognized as only Mr. Granger, she frowned and shook her head.

"Who is he, then?" she asked, looking back at Alex.

"He's my clone," Fisher pushed out. "I made him."

Veronica's eyes snapped back to Fisher's.

"You . . . made him?"

He nodded miserably. "In my home lab."

Amazingly, her eyes took on an expression of wonder.

"That's . . . incredible, Fisher," she said.

"I sent him to school . . . ," he went on.

"Because you couldn't take the way people treated you anymore," she said. He was so startled, he felt like she'd hit him with a miniature lightning bolt. "You were ignored, pushed around, beaten up. You didn't think you had any friends."

Fisher stared back at Veronica.

"Yes," he said. "That's exactly it. How . . . ?"

Veronica managed a small smile. "Fisher, it's amazing that you cloned yourself. But *why* you did it is pretty obvious." She shook her head. "Well, that explains why you'd occasionally act so strange and unlike yourself. You *weren't* yourself." Then she noticed Dr. X. "What about you, Mr. Granger? What are you doing here? I thought you retired."

"I am doing my best to help in this extremely dangerous endeavor," Dr. X replied.

Veronica's eyes narrowed quizzically for a few seconds, then got very wide.

"You're Dr. X," she said, with a breathy matter-of-factness.

This time, everyone turned to stare at her, including Dr. X himself.

"How . . . did you know that?" he asked.

"I could always tell something was off about you," said Veronica. "And I was always interested in the mysterious Dr. X. I watched all those videos, some many times. I watched *Family Feudalism*, too. When you started rambling on about your lost empire, most people just thought you were crazy. Deluded."

"That's not totally inaccurate . . . ," Alex pointed out.

"But not me," Veronica continued. "I *listened*." Her lips formed a triumphant smirk. "Now, seeing you here, is all the proof I need."

Fisher's jaw was doing its best to scrape up a mouthful of dirt from the yard. He'd been so concerned with how Veronica *felt* about him that he'd never spent a moment wondering what she *thought* about him—what she thought about *anything*.

"Wow," he said. "I'm . . . really impressed."

"That means a lot coming from someone who cloned himself," Veronica said with a grin. "So why are there Fisher-shaped robots all around? And why *is* he here?" She pointed to Dr. X.

"Because we need all the allies we can get," said Alex. "Even vicious, evil ones with unfortunately sized noses."

"It's regal!" said Dr. X, hoisting his nose in the air proudly.

"There's a third clone," said Fisher. "A clone that

Granger made. But he changed him, twisted him around. He's an emotionless villain. He's behind all of this. He made the Fisher-bots."

"And now we have to find him, and stop him," said Amanda, still eyeing Dr. X warily.

"All right," said Veronica, cracking her knuckles. "We've got no time to lose. You can fill in the details on the way."

# CHAPTER 16

*After much thinking, I've changed my mind.
The number of Fisher Bases on Earth should be limited
to one, or less.*

*—Dr. X, Personal Journal*

It was close to evening when the group set out. The sun was already dipping toward the horizon. Fisher wondered if he would ever see it rise again. It was a question he'd asked himself a few times too many for a twelve-year-old.

They'd have to pass through a small residential area. Then cross an open stretch along a larger road and past some stores and shopping areas, as well as the TechX ruin. Then they'd reach Wompalog.

"Did you ever get hold of Agent Mason?" said Amanda as she nudged Wally forward with a foot to keep him from chasing FP.

"No," Alex said grimly, shaking his head. "We have to assume we're on our own."

"*Almost* on our own." Fisher reached down and scratched Wally's chin, and the wombat started nuzzling his ankles. FP ran over and tried to push Wally aside with his head.

Fisher bent down and scooped up one animal in each arm. "We have a very important mission ahead of us and we all have to concentrate," he said, addressing the small mammals. "Are you both up to the task?"

FP snorted. Fisher swore he saw Wally salute.

"Okay, then," he said, putting the animals down. "First thing we have to do is get out of the neighborhood."

"Patrols are pretty light around here," Amanda said. "It's getting past the edge of the neighborhood on to the main road that leads to Wompalog that'll be tricky."

"Okay, then," said Alex. "Let's move."

Alex and Amanda took the lead, armed with the same electric stun sticks that Fisher and Alex had carried on the previous evening. They didn't know how well the weak zap would work against the Fisher-bots, but if the machines had poorly shielded circuits, the sticks might work even better on them than they did on humans.

Fisher and Veronica followed behind Amanda and Alex, sorting through the variety of equipment Fisher had packed into his bag to determine what would be most useful against the Fisher-bots and, eventually, Three. Dr. X took up the rear, his hands in his pockets, frowning deeply. Wally and FP flanked the group on both sides, like the cavalry screen of an ancient army.

There was nobody on the sidewalk, and no cars passed

down the street. Their footsteps were eerily loud against the neighborhood's silence. Fisher tried not to think of all that was riding on their mission. Now that Three had taken over, it would be a matter of days, if not hours, before those forces marched on Fisher's house and tore it to pieces, looking for him and Alex.

Fisher wouldn't let that happen.

Amanda and Alex ducked behind a parked car and motioned for the others to get down. Fisher and Veronica hid behind a second car and Dr. X crouched behind a blue USPS mailbox. Wally and FP noticed that everyone else had stopped and trotted back to Fisher.

Fisher-bots had fortified the street corner up ahead, which roughly marked the end of the neighborhood. Amanda crept back to talk to Fisher.

"Looks like they've cordoned off the whole area," she said. "They've got a guard post on the corner, with barriers blocking the street. I just saw some guy try and get through. They stopped him and checked his ID. One of them had some kind of scanner. Do you think they could be looking for you?"

Fisher didn't answer. He thought it likely. "How many are there?"

"Three," Amanda said. "There are probably other posts nearby, so if we take them out, we have to do it quietly."

"And all at the same time," Veronica said. "I'll lead this one."

"Why?" Fisher said, alarmed. The idea that Veronica was putting herself in harm's way made him feel queasy.

"They're not looking for me," she said. "Three doesn't know me. I'll set them up, and you can surround and ambush them."

Amanda nodded to her, and crept back up to whisper the plan to Alex. Fisher took his own stun stick from his bag.

"Keep watch here," Veronica whispered to Dr. X. "But be ready to help if we need it." The ex-overlord nodded.

"Okay, you two," Fisher said to FP and Wally. "Watch Dr. X. If he tries anything, bite his elbows off, okay?" The animals plunked down next to Dr. X with adorably tough looks on their faces.

The guard post was a bit more elaborate than the first one they'd seen, with a little booth next to the barriers going across the street. All three of the bots were outside, standing still, their gazes locked ahead.

"Excuse me?" Veronica said brightly, striding up to the checkpoint. "I was hoping you could help me find something. I'm trying to find the . . . oh, what's it called . . . it's like a coffee shop, but they have an electronics section, and a basement where they sell used clothing, so, like, you can drink your coffee as you look through clothes and Blu-ray players and stuff. . . ." As she spoke, she gesticulated in the general direction of downtown, and the Fisher-bots pivoted to watch her, giving Alex, Fisher, and Amanda the opportunity to move.

They moved silently up the street. Fisher steadied his grip around the stun stick. But the closer he got to the Fisher-bots, the dizzier he felt. He'd thought that having two clones would've made him used to seeing other hims walking around. But these were different. They stood completely motionless, their hands clasped behind their backs in their identical gray uniforms. He felt like he was looking at a mural.

Veronica was still blabbering. "I think it's on thirteenth, or maybe eighteenth, and it's got an old-fashioned wooden sign outside shaped like a rooster. . . ."

The Fisher-bots regarded her curiously, each looking like it wished to help her but could not. Fisher realized, suddenly, that they were charmed by her. Was Veronica actually flirting with these robots? Was Veronica so amazing that every single version of Fisher, no matter how robotic, would swoon when he saw her?

Either way, the Fisher-bots were completely distracted. At a nodded signal by Amanda, the three kids sprung. Fisher lunged forward and grasped the Fisher-bot by its shoulder. The bot started to turn in response, and Fisher caught a glimpse of a dead and bloodless mask of his own face. For a split second, he hesitated. The Fisher-bot shrugged his hand from its shoulder and reached for his throat.

Seeing the attack coming, Fisher stepped out of the way and jammed the stun stick into the bot's chest. The way the bot spasmed and flailed made him feel sicker than any nameless, semidissolved glop that the Wompalog cafeteria had ever served up. The stick overheated, sparked, and burned out just as the Fisher-bot fell to the ground, deactivated.

Fisher looked down at the bot. *It's just a machine,* he thought to himself. *Like a car or a lawn mower. A machine, with a Fisher paint job.*

All the Fisher-bots were now down, but the stun sticks were burned out and useless. Fisher, Amanda, and Alex abandoned them at the post, signaled Dr. X that the coast was clear, and moved on.

"Nice work," Amanda said to Veronica as they walked away. Veronica smiled.

They reached the main road that led straight to school. They kept as low as they could, staying concealed behind cars, trucks, storefronts, gas stations, trees—anything that could provide cover.

"Patrol," announced Amanda sharply.

The group dove behind two cars as five Fisher-bots marched past in perfect rhythm, gaze sweeping back and forth. Fisher tried to avoid looking at them. The more he

# How To Tell A Fisher-bot From The Real Thing:

- ~~Has trouble with eye contact~~
- ~~Uses incomprehensible words~~
- ~~Stiff, awkward posture~~
- Like Fisher but scary

looked at their eyes, the less he was able to think of them as machines. And if he had another moment's hesitation, it could cost them everything.

"Clear," Amanda said as the patrol receded behind them. "Let's hurry."

They ran down the road for nearly a quarter mile, until a familiar building came into view. It was Palo Alto's new King of Hollywood franchise, sitting happily atop the filled-in TechX crater. The spot where Fisher and Alex had discovered Three's abandoned hideout—exactly as Three had intended them to.

"Simply absurd," Dr. X muttered. "Where once my great monument to technological advancement and the triumph of the unconquerable human intellect once stood, now there is nothing but a monument to the immortality of the deep-frying process."

Everyone ignored him.

"How's it look?" Fisher asked Alex, who was doing reconnaissance with a small gadget he'd made: it resembled a highlighter pen but was actually a powerful telescope.

"It looks like it's still operating. I see workers . . . wait a minute. Take a look."

Alex handed Fisher the telescope.

There were, indeed, five people inside, wearing the bright blue-and-green shirts and caps of King of Hollywood employees. And they were all exactly the same size. After a minute, Fisher glimpsed two of their faces.

"Bots," he said. "All of them."

"Is there anyone else in there?" said Amanda.

"Negative," said Fisher, after taking a few more seconds to scan the place through the wide windows all along its walls. "But it looks like they're set up with binoculars, cameras, and communications equipment."

"It's a surveillance post," said Alex. "We'll have to go pretty far out of our way if we have any hope of getting past them undetected."

"Let's take them out," said Amanda.

"And burn the whole cursed place down," said Dr. X, smacking his staff into his palm and staring hatefully at the fast-food joint. Not long ago, he'd schemed to use

AGH to bring the whole chain down on the head of its owner, who'd tormented him in school. "Burn it. Burn it *all*!"

"No," Veronica said firmly. "Destroying the building will attract every android in town right to us. If we're going to take out the bots, we have to be quick about it. And quiet."

"Any suggestions on how we do that?" said Fisher.

Veronica took the telescope and peered out at the King of Hollywood for a couple of minutes.

"Right," she said, giving the scope back to Fisher and searching his backpack for a pen and a notepad. "Here's the plan. . . ."

Veronica walked into the King of Hollywood through its sleek, automatic sliding door. Three Fisher-bots stood behind the counter. Two bots moved mops back and forth endlessly on the same two square feet of floor. Fisher had given her a little microphone disguised as an earring. He'd designed it several weeks ago for Amanda, in case she'd needed to reprise her role as J. Nadine Weathersby, Fisher's "attorney."

"Hi," Veronica said, walking up to the counter. "I'd like to order a small wombat to go."

The bots blinked at her blankly.

"We are very sorry," one of them said, in a clipped

mechanical voice. "We do not know the meaning of *wombat*."

Veronica smiled. "How silly of me," she said. "I'll show you." She gave a sharp whistle, and Wally and FP darted into the building, scrambling in quick loops around the restaurant. The Fisher-bots on cleaning duty dropped their mops to chase the animals.

Wally and FP bolted out of the King of Hollywood and into the parking lot again, with the two Fisher-bots in pursuit.

Fisher, Dr. X, Alex, and Amanda sprang.

Fisher pulled one to the ground and Dr. X delivered the coup de grace with his staff. Alex and Amanda grabbed the other. Three fistfuls of wires later, each was reduced to a lifeless metal and fake flesh shell.

Inside the King of Hollywood, Veronica was slowly backing away from the counter. "So do you *have* wombats?" she said as the remaining Fisher-bots began to slowly advance toward her. "No? Okay . . . I guess I'll have some popcorn."

She threw herself to the side as Fisher burst in the door with the others behind him, his trusty popcorn gun in his hands.

He felt like Vic Daring charging against the subterranean machine hordes of Mars, his movie snack–powered weapon jolting and bucking in his hands as it spat a steady stream of singeing-hot kernels at the Fisher-bots. The new, extra-butter rounds made the tile floor slick, and the bots slipped as they charged at Fisher and thudded to the ground.

It was easy enough for Dr. X, Amanda, and Alex to finish them off as Fisher coolly dropped the empty popcorn gun, breathing out in exultant triumph.

"You're quite a tactician," Amanda said to Veronica.

"Strategy has always been one of my favorite parts of history to study," Veronica answered. "Alexander the Great, Napoleon, Ulysses S. Grant. I guess I picked up something from them."

Fisher felt a warm flush in his chest. She was even more amazing than he'd ever known.

But as they turned to leave the King of Hollywood, a triumphal march filled their ears. They swiveled in unison. In one corner of the restaurant, one of Three's holographic message pods activated, projecting his image into space. His eyes were hidden behind his cap brim.

"Hello again, dear citizens." Three's voice resonated from the speakers. "It has come to my attention that there are certain dangerous criminals on the loose among us. They seek to tear down the newly restored order, and plunge us once more into chaos. Rest assured, I am taking steps to quell these outbursts of uncivilized behavior."

The image shifted. Three's face broke apart, and the projector cut to a Palo Alto street, in which dozens of Fisher-bots were amassing.

"Fisher . . . ," Alex said. He raised a trembling finger to point.

Fisher felt as though he had inhaled a bag of dust.

"You can expect that, within the hour," continued Three, "all remaining forces of chaos will be dealt with. Completely."

The transmission winked out, but the last few seconds of footage kept playing in Fisher's mind: easily a hundred Fisher-bots standing in tight ranks like a Roman legion, right outside his house.

"We have to go back," said Alex, ghost white. "Mom and Dad are at home. They'll never be able to fend off an attack."

He was already headed to the door.

"Alex, *wait*!" Fisher said. Alex turned back, desperation in his eyes. "We have to take Three down. Don't you see? That's the best way to help Mom and Dad. Even if we went back now, how can we stop a hundred Fisher-bots?"

"We have to try," Alex spat out, his words harsh like jets of flame. "What if we don't get to Three in time? He said, 'within the hour.' They could be breaking through the Liquid Door right now!"

"And what if it's a trap?" Fisher fired back. "Three's

been two steps ahead of us all this time. He knew we'd see the broadcast. And he must know we're on the hunt. What if this is a setup to lure us back to the house, where he can crush us?"

"Well, what if Wompalog *is* a trap?" Alex said. "What if he knew that we'd want revenge after we saw what he had planned for Mom and Dad? What if we're walking straight into his clutches?"

"*Both* ways are a trap," Veronica's voice cut in. She stepped between the brothers. "Either way, Three's got something big waiting for us." She turned to Alex and put a hand on his shoulder. "Fisher's right. If we go back now, we'll be fighting against impossible odds. But if we stop Three, we stop everything."

Alex took a moment to stare at the floor. He composed himself and looked at Fisher with a much softer expression.

"I haven't even gotten used to the feeling of having parents yet," he said, nearly pleading. "I can't lose them now."

"You won't," said Fisher. "I promise. But we have to move, and we have to move *fast*."

They ran out of the King of Hollywood.

"Any transportation ideas?" Amanda said.

"Maybe," said Alex. "This road goes downhill all the way to Wompalog. Fisher, you still have that inflatable family thing?"

"The IRATE?" he said. "Yeah."

"It's on wheels, right?" said Alex.

Fisher allowed himself a small smile. "Well, this should be fun."

"Mom! Mom! Mom! Mom! Ice cream!"

"I hate this place! Why can't we go to Maui?"

"Everyone, calm down. I'm getting a migraine!"

"This castle is four hundred years old! Feel the history!"

The IRATE rolled along the downhill street at a frightening pace as Fisher, Alex, Amanda, Veronica, and Dr. X clung to it for dear life. The IRATE's central control wasn't much wider than a skateboard, and it leaned dangerously far left and right as its unexpected passengers adjusted their weight.

"Left!" Fisher said, holding on to the boy on the left side. "Lean toward me!" FP sat on top of the father's head, his ears flattened back by the wind, squealing happily. Wally, who was nestled in the mother's arms, just on top of one of the wailing babies, clamped his paws over his eyes.

"What?" shouted Alex. "I can't hear you!"

"Doesn't this have a volume control??" said Dr. X, his arm snaked around the mother's waist.

"More speed, Alex!" shouted Amanda, clinging to

the father. Alex unscrewed his Instant Ice thermos and tossed some of it onto the street in front of them. It froze the moment it struck asphalt, and the IRATE lurched forward.

The school was coming into view. Immediately, Fisher could tell that something was wrong. He didn't know what, exactly—he was still too far away to make out more than the broad outlines of the building.

A tall hedge bordered the sidewalk to their right. He pointed to it wildly.

"Bail out! Bail out!!" he shouted at the top of his lungs.

Alex leaned as far out as he could to steer them to the right side of the street, and then leapt into the hedge. The rest of the group followed him. Fisher grabbed FP and tucked him under his arm like a football before jumping.

Fisher had the blissful, utterly free sensation of a soaring eagle for about one and a quarter seconds. Then he felt the enthusiastic embrace of dozens of bristly, spiny twigs, and found himself nose to formidable nose with Dr. X. The air went out of his chest at once. Suddenly, he felt more like a porcupine victim than an eagle.

"Everyone okay?" Amanda said, her voice muffled in the leaves. A series of grunts sounded in reply. In the background, the IRATE's endless babbling went on as it careened toward Wompalog without them.

"Everyone, calm down. I'm getting a migraine!"

"This castle is four hundred years—"

*BOOOOOOOM.*

Fisher scrambled out of the hedge and peeked around it. The IRATE had rolled right up to Wompalog's main entrance . . . and exploded. It was now a smoking heap of plastic and metal.

The others dug themselves free of the foliage and took a look themselves.

"Fisher . . . ," Veronica said, her voice tight with fear. She didn't have to finish her sentence.

Overnight, Wompalog had become a fortress.

Two rows of tall chain-link fence topped with barbed wire surrounded the entire school. Several Fisher-bots were posted on the rooftop with binoculars, and dozens patrolled the grounds below. Some of them carried weapons that looked like the blade, club, and whip attachments Dr. X's robots had used in LA. There were concrete fortifications on the sidewalks outside with even bigger weapons.

They had no time to reconsider their plan. The clock was ticking. Even now Fisher's parents could be under attack.

"Do you think they know we're here?" Amanda said, watching as several bots moved forward to inspect what was left of the IRATE.

"Probably not," said Veronica. "But they know something's

wrong. We won't be able to sneak past all those guards."

"All right. But if you kids are all so smart, tell me: how *do* we get in?" said Dr. X. "All we've got is an amateur wrestler, an even more amateur general, an evil genius, a pair of quadrupeds, and . . . you two," he said, pointing at Fisher and Alex. Then he cocked his head, squinting slightly. "You two . . ."

"What is it?" said Alex. "What're you thinking?"

"I am thinking," said Dr. X, "of how you two would look in gray."

# ≋ CHAPTER 17 ≋

We were pretty sure we'd found Three's base.
But while finding a dragon's cave is all well and good,
you've still got to walk into it.

                              —Fisher Bas, Personal Notes

The Fisher-bots circled Wompalog endlessly, without tiring. The majority of the force stuck close to the school, but
after the IRATE's explosive crash, two of them were moving in wider and wider loops. Fisher had hastily calculated
that within two minutes, the bots would pass between a
school bus and the hedge that they were hiding behind.
Then they would be out of sight from the rest of the bots
for exactly six seconds.

It was almost time.

"That's our opening," said Fisher. "Amanda, are you
ready?"

"Of course," she said, cracking her knuckles. "Just tell
me when."

"Here they come," said Alex, peering through a gap in
the hedge. The patrolling Fisher-bots were crossing the
street. Amanda inched forward. "Almost . . ." The bots
moved down the sidewalk. In a few more seconds, they'd

be behind the bus. She crouched, clenching and unclenching her fists. *"Now!"*

Amanda leapt out from the hedge, catching both Fisher-bots off guard. She threw one over her hip and levered the other down with an armlock. Alex, Fisher, and Veronica jumped out to help, but by the time they reached Amanda, she had both bots under control. Both were struggling on their stomachs. She had their hands bent up around her ankles.

"Nice hold," Fisher said as he and Alex knelt down, opened the access panels on the Fisher-bots' necks and pulled out their main control lines.

"It's a medieval move," Amanda said proudly. "Picked it up from a fifteenth-century German fighting book."

"They clearly don't communicate by wireless transmission, or they could instantly alert one another when attacked," said Dr. X. "And the others would be swarming us by now."

"But they must be receiving a master signal," Fisher. "How else would Three coordinate them so fast?"

"Well, of course, dear boy," said Dr. X, for a second sounding like the old Harold Granger. "They just cannot communicate with *each other* that way. It's a way of ensuring loyalty and discouraging independent thinking. Trust me. I invented a similar system myself."

FP approached the Fisher-bots cautiously, sniffed at

one, and shrank away with a faint squeak.

"All right, let's work quickly," Alex said, stripping the bots of their uniforms. Underneath the clothing, they looked like store-bought mannequins. "When the patrol doesn't report back in time, the other Fisher-bots will want to know why. Let's make sure we've got an answer for them."

Fisher pulled on one gray outfit and Alex climbed into the other. The uniforms were roomy enough to fit over the snug-fitting spy suits, and covered them completely.

"How do we look?" Fisher asked Amanda.

"Good. Just try to act emotionally uncertain and unable to relate to human beings," she said. "Fisher, that shouldn't be as hard for you." She grinned.

Fisher stuck his tongue out in reply as he smoothed his sleeves. He knew she was only half joking, but he also knew that his ability to relate to human beings was far greater than it used to be. He'd gotten a lot of help from the clone formerly known as Two.

"Hang on," said Veronica, taking a comb from her back pocket and fixing Fisher's and Alex's hair. Fisher nearly melted to a puddle when he felt her fingers in her hair. Alex pinched him sharply.

"There," she said. "Now you look perfect."

"Try to keep your voices flat and toneless," Dr. X said.

"Fisher," Amanda said, "that should be easy for—"

"Oh, shut up," Fisher said, smiling. "And put these on." He had found a bundle of ratcheting plastic zip ties in one pocket that would serve very well as simple handcuffs.

Two minutes later, Fisher and Alex emerged from behind the bus. Alex marched in front, carrying Dr. X's staff, and Fisher took up the back. The rest of the crew was cuffed between them. Fisher tried to walk as stiffly as he could, and his nervousness definitely helped. He had FP under one arm and Wally under the other.

Alex led the group in the direction of the front door, keeping his knees straight and his face expressionless. Fisher was thankful that the animals under his own arms weren't struggling. The other bots acknowledged them, but didn't approach.

So far, their plan was working.

Alex raised an arm stiffly in the air, signaling to the other guards.

"Prisoners," Alex said, in the deadest voice Fisher had ever heard him use. His expression was as perfectly rigid as those of the Fisher-bots. Maybe he'd picked up a few acting tricks while he'd been in LA.

There were several guards posted in front of the school's double doors. One of the guards looked over Amanda, Veronica, and Dr. X.

A few seconds of silence passed. Beads of sweat started to form on Fisher's skin. If he started to sweat, his robot disguise would be ruined. The thought wasn't helping. He felt the diabolical camera eyes on him, sweeping, prying, evaluating.

"These are key targets," the bot responded in an equally cold voice that made Fisher exert extra effort to keep from shuddering. "They may have important information. Detain them inside."

Fisher swallowed back a sigh of relief.

The Fisher-bots at the front doors nodded and allowed the group to proceed.

Wompalog's main hallway was totally silent. Most of the lights were off, and afternoon light fading from gold to orange streaked along the floor and left long, warped shadows across the gaping lockers and overturned garbage cans in the hall. The notes of the on-strike teachers still clung to classroom doors, and a single pencil rolled along the floor, disturbed by the sound of the doors slamming shut.

Veronica walked up to what Fisher remembered was the door to her fifth-period French class. He knew it well, because he'd tried to be at his locker nearby every day when the class got out, just so he could see her. Back then he could barely gibber out a hello to her before tripping over his own shins.

Now they were saving the world together.

"It's so creepy in here," she said in a whisper.

# FORT WOMPALOG
## occupied by
## Three and Fisher-bots

NOT TO SCALE

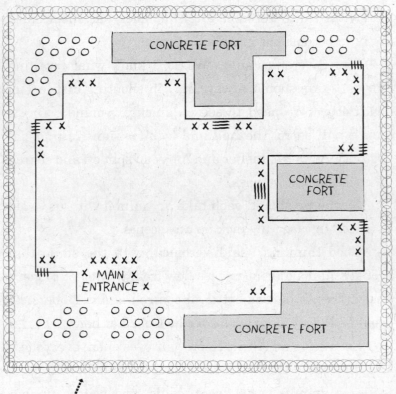

CONCRETE FORT

CONCRETE FORT

CONCRETE FORT

MAIN ENTRANCE

chain link fence
with barbed wire

X = Fisher-bots on roof
O = Fisher-bots on ground

Alex took out a small pocketknife and used it to cut the zip ties. He handed Dr. X back his staff. Fisher put down the animals, who started sniffing around the hall immediately. But they didn't turn up anything more interesting than a crumpled, empty bag of Bugles.

"Let's go get him," said Amanda. The others instinctively turned to Veronica after a moment, as she seemed to have become the group's tactician.

"Okay," Veronica said. "We don't know what's waiting for us, so we should always stay in shouting distance of each other. We need to search quickly. Amanda, Dr. X, and I will patrol the hall and look for signs of unusual activity. As we go, Fisher and Alex can split off and search the classrooms we pass."

"Maybe we should each take an animal with us," said Fisher. "In case they pick up any scents."

"Good thinking," said Veronica, with the smile that could still make heat ripples flow from the top of Fisher's head. Even if he was better at controlling his gibbers, he could still feel them whenever he looked at her.

"Let's go," said Alex. "Keep your eyes open, everyone."

They paced their way slowly along the hall, searching lockers, scanning the floors, walls, and ceiling. Fisher couldn't help but imagine his mom and dad, dragged out of the house by mechanical monsters bearing his own face. The image fueled him with anger. He had to remind himself that being thorough was just as important as being quick.

At the first set of classrooms, Fisher and Alex peeled off from the group. Fisher and FP went left. It was an eighth-grade classroom, but it looked pretty much like all the others. A few desks had books on them and Fisher turned each over in case some small clue might pop up. FP sniffed along the floor and around the chairs and desks.

The blackboard was covered with writing in thick chalk. There was so much of it overlapping that he couldn't tell what any of it had once said.

"Keep looking around, boy," he said as he approached the board. He puzzled at it, eyebrows furrowed. Could there be a message here? He took hold of the eraser in the center of the board's shelf.

And he heard a click.

He barely had time to dive away from the board as its entire surface began to vibrate faster than a dentist's drill. The vibration threw the whole thick coat of chalk on its surface into the air as a dense, suffocating cloud. Fisher grabbed FP by the tail and scrambled out of the room, his hand clamped over his mouth and nose. He collapsed outside the door, gasping for breath, FP next to him, sneezing nonstop.

"Fisher!" Veronica said, dropping to his side. "Are you all right?"

"Fine," Fisher said, with a slight cough. "I don't think it was poisoned. Just regular chalk dust. But there was an awful lot of it."

He stood up and brushed himself off as Alex and Wally emerged from the room across the hall unscathed.

"Everything all right?" he said.

"Yeah," Fisher said. "I think that one was just to scare me. And it worked."

The next few classrooms yielded nothing. The quiet was starting to weigh heavily on them. Halfway down the hall, they came to the old, wooden double doors of the library.

"I'll go first," Amanda said, easing the door open.

Fisher realized he'd never actually heard the library quiet before. There weren't any kids throwing small objects and bits of petrified food back and forth; nobody was trying to climb the bookshelves; nobody was dropping dictionaries on his head from above.

The library was a big, circular room. Dust swam in the sunlight that got through the old, chipped windows. Rows of shelves, arranged in a semicircle, dominated most of the room.

"Looks peaceful enough," said Dr. X.

"Let's do a quick search," said Amanda. "We've got a lot of ground left to cover."

Fisher led FP far into the stacks, running his hand

along the book spines, occasionally checking behind one that looked out of place or at a different angle from the others. The others split up to look around the reference desk and the computers. FP whined a little, and Fisher reached down to scoop him up.

"We're doing our best, boy," he said. FP kept whining as the rest of the crew caught up to them.

"Anything?" said Alex.

"Nothing," said Fisher. "FP, would you please stop . . ."

Then he heard something, like a faint series of clanks. FP whined a little louder. The others froze.

Then a single, great *clank* shook the floor.

"Run," Alex breathed out, barely above a whisper.

The world came crashing down.

Every single eight-foot-high bookshelf in the library began toppling as if a well-coordinated team of invisible giants were shoving them over. The way out of the stacks was impassable. They barely got out of the space they'd been in before one huge shelf smashed into the other and sent it reeling in turn.

The shelves fell in all directions, like dominoes that could push back. They fell forward, back, left, right, in ways that shouldn't have been possible. Then Fisher realized: the shelves *weren't* just falling. They were *moving*. Three's technology was at work here. Each shelf had an antigravity generator attached to its underside. They could hover a few inches above the ground and move at will.

They could go on the attack.

The group ducked one way and dodged another, leaping over the tons of oak that splintered to the floor all around them.

A huge shelf unit crashed to the floor, and cut Fisher, FP, and Veronica off from the rest of the group. Fisher looked through a tiny gap at Alex.

"We can't get to you!" he shouted above the apocalyptic din.

"We'll find our own way out!" Alex screamed back. "Save yourselves!"

Two massive shelves were teetering toward them. Fisher spun around, searching for a way out. There were obstacles behind them and on both sides. If these two shelves fell on them, they'd be completely trapped, assuming they even survived the impact.

"Fisher!" Veronica screamed, unable to get anything else out.

Then Fisher spotted something bolted to the ceiling ahead. It was a steel bar used to mount a projector.

He whipped his elastic necktie from his backpack and offered it to FP, who clamped it firmly in his mouth. Then Fisher pointed to the bar.

"Through the hoop, boy!" he said. "And I hope you find our friends on the other side!"

Fisher lifted FP over his head, drew his arms back as far as he could, and threw the pig with all of his strength. FP sailed into the air and opened up his foreleg gliding wings. He sped between the bar and the ceiling, the stretchy tie trailing him. It folded around the bar and disappeared out of sight.

The shelves began to tip.

*"Fisher!"* He heard Alex bellow. *"We've got it! Go!!"*

Fisher gave the tie a quick tug, and the bar held firm.

"Hold on," he said to Veronica. He stepped back as far as he could, and the tie stretched even more, like an expanding spring. Veronica grasped the tie with one hand, and put her other arm around Fisher's waist. Then she gave him a hasty peck on the cheek.

"For luck," she said, with a terrified smile. Fisher felt a rush of heat. Veronica's arm was like a magic belt of courage around his waist.

"Three steps," he rushed out as the shelves began to fall. "Then jump!"

The tie pulled them forward as they took three running steps and then leapt as hard as they could. The tie held. They were airborne. Air blew past Fisher's face, and Veronica's arm tightened almost too much for him to breathe. His trailing foot cleared the top of a falling shelf by less than an inch.

And then they were out. They saw Amanda, Dr. X,

and Alex holding on to the tie with all of their strength. Slowly, it stretched out again, and lowered Fisher and Veronica to the floor. The crashing sounds had stopped. Everything that could fall had fallen. Fisher and Veronica let go and collapsed. FP ran over and started nuzzling and licking Fisher's face.

"That's . . . the third time you've saved my life, boy," Fisher said, scratching the little pig's head. "I'm glad you accept thanks in popcorn. I'll make sure we never run out again."

# CHAPTER 18

*I can't count the number of times I've saved your bacon.*
                    *—Hal Torque, brief sidekick to Vic Daring*

*I guess it shouldn't surprise me that you can't count to two.*
                    *—Vic Daring, Issue #129*

Alex helped Fisher up. Amanda lent Veronica an arm.

"I say we make for the science lab," Alex said. "We need to double our firepower, quick."

"Sounds good," said Fisher. "Let's hurry."

They ran out of the library and down the hall. FP and Wally kept up, their little legs pounding the tile floor like pistons.

"Down!" Amanda shouted. As one, the group crouched, just in time for a hail of extremely sharp number 2 pencils to spit from the lockers on their left and smack into those on the right. Fisher noticed a broken piece of thin, clear wire on the floor. Amanda must have tripped it.

"Clear!" she shouted, and they moved on.

They took a left turn at the hallway that would take them to the science lab, their eyes shifting back and forth, looking for the next trap.

"Heads up!" came Amanda's commanding voice as the squeak of wheels sounded from the end of the hall.

"Is that . . . ," said Alex.

"Yeah," said Amanda, her eyes widening with dread. "Cafeteria cart."

"I guess all the best artists steal ideas," Alex said as the cart barreled along toward them. Mounted on the cart, rigged to face forward, were eight toasters. The powerful smell of smoke and carbon residue assaulted their nostrils.

Fisher had seen at least one kid break a molar on the cafeteria's toast, so he knew enough to take the threat seriously.

"To the side!" Amanda shouted as a rapid *clink-clink-clink-clink-clink-clink* filled the hallway. Fisher threw himself left with Veronica and Alex as Dr. X and Amanda went right. The projectiles sailed past them—charred, withered pieces of what could be called bread in the same way that a puddle of crude oil could be called a dinosaur.

The blackened toast bullets whizzed safely past, but the cart barreled on toward them. And now two more carts came into view close behind. The first had nearly reached them when Dr. X shouted to Fisher.

"Fisher! The tie! Throw me the tie!"

Fisher did, so that the tie stretched across the hallway.

"Everyone, hold tight!" Dr. X shouted. Amanda got a

# Schematics for
# ATTACK TOASTER

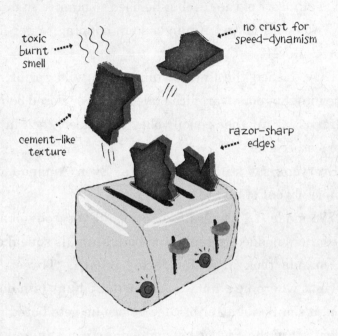

toxic burnt smell ......

no crust for speed-dynamism ......

cement-like texture ......

razor-sharp edges ......

firm grip on his end of the tie as Alex and Veronica added their efforts to Fisher's.

The cart hit the tie, and Fisher strained against the pressure. The cart stretched the tie out, and out, and out . . . until finally, it could stretch no more. Then all of that wound-up energy was released in a deafening snap as the tie, like a giant slingshot, catapulted the cart back the way it had come, crashing into the other two and landing all three of them in a pile of spinning wheels and squeaking axles.

"Good work," said Dr. X, and Fisher, for just an instant, saw a glimmer of the teacher he used to admire so much.

"Two doors down," Amanda said, hopping to her feet. "Move! Move!"

They dashed the final distance in a wild sprint and dove into the room. Veronica pulled the door closed behind them just as another pencil volley embedded itself in the door's other side.

Everyone sat still for a minute. Even Amanda was completely out of breath.

"We made it," Alex said, panting. "Everybody okay?" The others nodded in reply, and both animals squeaked.

Amanda took in a shuddering breath. "Three's got us right where he wants us. If we don't hunt him down soon, it's only a matter of time before he gets bored and orders all of the Fisher-bots outside to come in and finish us off."

"Yes," said Veronica, opening Ms. Snapper's desk drawers and rifling through them. "This *is* exactly how Three wants us. Running, tired, scared, not thinking before we act. We need to calm down and restrategize."

"We don't have that kind of time," Amanda argued. "For all we know, a hundred Fisher-bots are about to kick down that door right now."

"And *our* door, Fisher," Alex said, standing up and rifling through a chemical storage cabinet, the very cabinet that Fisher had once hidden in to escape the Vikings. Back when there was no Two, let alone Three, and Dr. X had been meek, friendly Mr. Granger.

"But if we don't take a moment to get organized," Fisher said, "we'll never find him, and we're doomed, anyway."

*"Wait!"* said Dr. X. Everyone turned to look at him as he scratched his beak of a nose in thought. "You are both correct. On the one hand, simply running around blindly, hoping to bump into Three is a foolish plan. On the other, our position here in the middle of his forces is not the place to stop and regroup. However, I can offer a compromise. A way to find out what we need, and quickly."

"Go on," said Fisher, raising an eyebrow suspiciously.

Dr. X walked over to the glass tank where Einy and Berg scurried around. As soon as they saw him, they started clambering at the wall. He opened the top and they scurried up onto his arms.

"Einstein and Heisenberg are not ordinary mice," Dr. X explained. "I modified them with several genes from other species. Including scent genes from a bloodhound." He lifted them to his face and they pawed at his cheeks affectionately. "They could track a freshly bathed, hairless

215

cat through a mountain pass in the middle of a blizzard. If Three is here, they will find him."

Dr. X held the mice out to Fisher and let them smell him, then did the same with Alex. He held them near his face as he walked over to a small air vent, holding them in one hand and petting them with the other. Then he made a series of complex chittering sounds at them. They seemed to understand, and took off through the vent.

"You . . . speak mouse?" Amanda said.

"Yes, of course," said Dr. X, deadly serious. But his frown started to crack, and he broke into hearty laughter. "Don't be silly. Mice don't have a language. But I find if you make sounds like theirs, they're more inclined to like you."

He chuckled.

Someone else chuckled, too.

Fisher looked around. No one else was laughing.

The chuckling was coming from *above* them.

Suddenly, the plaster ceiling tiles at the far end of the room burst apart into chips and dust as a person fell through them, landing on a lab table and knocking over a set of beakers.

Einy and Berg were crawling all over him, tickling him with their paws. He managed to flick them off, and stood up to his full height. He wasn't any taller than Alex or Fisher, but there was a menacing power to him that made him seem six feet tall.

And his eyes. His terrible, wintry eyes, which made Fisher feel like a bacterium under a microscope.

"Looks like you got me," said Three, baring his teeth, which looked sharp enough to slice through leather. "Exactly as I had planned."

# ≋ CHAPTER 19 ≋

*It's tough being the middle child. Especially when the eldest grew you in a tube and the youngest tried to kill you.*

—Alex Bas, Journal

"I suppose this wouldn't be the best time to point out you just crushed a very valuable set of beakers," said Dr. X. "Imported. Do you know how much it costs to ship glass?"

Fisher looked to Amanda and Alex. Their faces were set and grim. Veronica's eyes were wide, her expression taut with fear.

This was it. The chance to end it.

Or the chance that Three would end it.

"I'm impressed," said Three. "You've gotten farther than I expected you to." He held some kind of remote in one hand—probably the way he was controlling the Fisher-bots. "I've been here for some time, living in the rafters and ducts, out of sight. Watching all of you go about your purposeless lives. Slowly working up a plan to exploit your weak, bendable minds. With the resources available to me after I deposed Dr. X, it was easy enough to purchase an unused factory building in a distant, remote location and remake it to serve my purposes.

"And while my army was under construction, I was content to make my hiding place here. Before leaving Los Angeles, I had attached my signal-hacking device to the studio broadcasting *Family Feudalism*. Once in hiding here, I activated it, observing the havoc my mind-altering signal worked, up close and personally."

Three's thumb made a subtle move on the control remote. Faintly, through the school's walls, Fisher heard footsteps. Hundreds of footsteps.

Suddenly, a Vic Daring storyline in which Vic accidentally unleashed a rapidly multiplying insect army, and then had to spend months fighting against it and repairing the damage it caused, popped into Fisher's head. At the end of the story, Vic was banished from the planet where he had wreaked all the havoc. The key difference between that situation and this one, Fisher thought, was that Fisher didn't have any other planets to go to.

"What is it you want?" Amanda said, giving Three a searing glare. "Why have you done all of this?"

"Ah," Three said. "This is the part where you expect me to make a speech like the one my former master"—he inclined his head toward Dr. X—"made not long ago. Explaining his painful past, the mistreatment he suffered from others, and how that drove him to seek vengeance on the world."

Dr. X stiffened, glaring.

"But now you can understand the difference between him and me," Three continued. "I have no past wrongs, because I have no past. Dr. X did what he did because people hurt his poor, weak feelings. He wanted to prove himself. I, on the other hand, am not driven by passion, or the need for revenge. He will never be as dangerous or powerful as I can be, for the simple reason that I don't seek to gain power and control because I was driven to it. I seek power and control simply because I can."

FP and Wally were growling, but Fisher could tell from the way FP's ears were batting back and forth that he was afraid. He'd never been this close to Three before.

Fisher's legs felt like stone as Three's almost hypnotic, machinelike voice filled his head. In a way, it was Fisher's own outburst of vengeful anger that had brought Two, and then Three, into the world. Fisher remembered the white-hot need for revenge and acceptance that had once run through him. He might have ended up like Dr. X.

"And now," Three said, "my bots are inside the school, closing in on this very room. They'll be here in just a few minutes. So, if you'd all like to—"

Amanda lost what little self-control she'd had left. With no warning, she burst forward and charged at Three. Fisher would sooner have stood in front of a logging truck with its brakes cut than try to stop Amanda on a mission.

Three, however, didn't bat an eye. He dropped into a crouch, and they locked arms like a pair of reindeer clashing antlers. She shot low, trying to get an arm around his front leg and trip him. He deftly shifted his feet out of her reach, wrapped one wrist around her reaching arm, and grabbed the back of her shirt with his other hand. He twisted his hips and threw her off her feet, sending her into the floor with a smack.

Amanda, dazed from the landing, was unable to get back to her feet. Three laughed.

"Stay . . . away . . . from . . . her," Alex spat out, between gritted teeth. He whipped something out of his bag that looked like a cross between a 1950s sci-fi ray gun, a sophisticated computer system, and a really evil food processor. He took hold of it, pointed its maniacally barbed barrel at Three, and eased his finger over the trigger.

Fisher turned to Alex, fear on his face.

"Wait, Alex! Not yet! Not yet!!"

But Alex didn't listen. *"This is for throwing me to the squiranhas!"* he shouted, pulling the trigger. The weapon started to shake, and so did Alex.

"Hold on!" Fisher said, terror rising in its voice. "It's almost charged! Just a few more seconds!"

"I . . . I . . . ," Alex said, his teeth chattering as the shaking grew more severe. "I . . . *eaaaghhhh!*" He collapsed, dropping the weapon to the floor, his body convulsing.

# Schematics for
# THE SECRET WEAPON

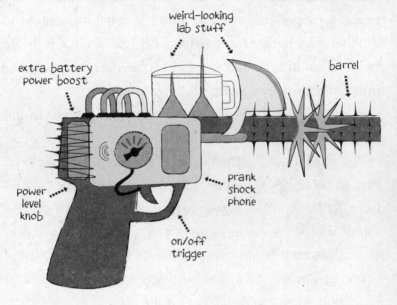

weird-looking
lab stuff

extra battery
power boost

barrel

power
level
knob

prank
shock
phone

on/off
trigger

"I . . . I'm sorry, Fisher. I . . . couldn't handle the . . . feed-back." He gasped and shuddered as Three let out a dry chuckle.

"What a nice-looking toy," he said, picking up the weapon. "What does it do?"

"No," Fisher said as he, Veronica, and Dr. X backed up to the wall. Amanda was still on the floor, clutching her head. The footsteps in the hall had grown deafening.

Three narrowed his eyes. "Careless of you to employ a weapon you aren't strong enough to handle." He spotted the weapon's power-level knob. "Not even at twenty-five percent. Why don't we try one hundred percent? See just what this creation of yours is capable of."

He pointed the weapon down at Alex.

"This is what I should've done the first time, instead of messing around with silly fish."

Three pulled the trigger. . . .

And fell down like a stack of empty tissue boxes in a wind tunnel. His body jerked and spasmed as it hit the floor. Amanda and Alex were up instantly, and Fisher leapt in to join them as Amanda grabbed Three's arms and Alex held his legs. Fisher knelt on Three's back and put two of the zip ties in his pocket around his wrists and two more around his ankles.

Veronica stared, dumbfounded.

"What happened?" she said.

"It's not a gun," said Fisher. "It's one of those trick phones that zaps you when you touch it. Alex and I added an on/off trigger and a power knob, replaced the wiring and the battery to make it eight times more powerful, then stuck a bunch of whatever weird-looking things we had lying around the lab onto it. We knew Three wouldn't be able to resist it."

But before they could celebrate their victory, the door

behind them shook and rattled. The bots were charging the door. They heard wood splinter. One more hit like that and the door would be off its hinges.

"Hurry," Fisher said to Alex. "Let me see that controller. We have destroy it and turn off those bots before they break in here, and into our house."

"I don't have it," Alex said, with panic in his voice. "I thought you did."

"And I thought . . . ," Fisher trailed off.

There was a delicate cough behind him.

With a sinking feeling, Fisher turned around.

Dr. X had the controller. And as the Fisher-bots burst in to surround them, his sickle-sharp smile told them his evil side was very much back.

# ≋ CHAPTER 20 ≋

knock, knock . . . Nobody's there, the knocking was just to
distract you while I cut through the wall. . . .
You see? I am not entirely humorless.

—Three, Audio Log

"Hmm," Dr. X said, examining the controller as Fisher-
bots continued to flow into the room. "Interesting. An
intuitive yet sophisticated control device. I recognize the
signature of technologies I developed at TechX, but there
are some modifications." His smile was cold, and Fisher
felt its coldness seep into the air around him. It took him
right back to the moment he'd first seen Dr. X in person.
That is, Dr. X *as* Dr. X. He'd seen him in person as Harold
Granger nearly every day before that.

He often went back in his mind, searching through
his memories to see if there was any way he could have
known, if there were clues he'd missed. So far, all he'd
come up with was the fact that Mr. Granger had been
very quiet, absorbed in his work, and lacking friends.
Qualities Fisher had shared.

It wasn't a very reassuring thought.

"Hey, uh . . . Alex?" Fisher said, as the twenty or thirty

Fisher-bots surrounded them, in response to Dr. X's manipulations.

"Yeah," Alex responded

"Did our clever secret plan include provisions for this?"

"Nope," Alex mumbled.

"Thought so. Just checking," Fisher said.

"You see, Fisher?" said Dr. X, holding the controller like it was a cup of tea. "You can never trust anyone. Not really. And you can never rely on anyone else to help you. There is only power, and opportunity." He gestured at the room around them with his free hand.

"Just think about your time here at school. You created this . . . *copy* of yourself . . . because you were unliked and unlikeable, invisible to those you wished could see you and a bright red target to those you wished you could escape. Then your situation changed dramatically. But why? Ask yourself, truly, why?"

Fisher looked around at the others. Amanda, scowling. Veronica, frightened but resolute, her jaw set. Alex, trying to keep an eye on the restrained Three, who was just starting to wake up. And all those Fisher-bots, staring blankly at him as they awaited their orders.

"Suddenly, you gained influence. Prestige. Popularity. Why? Because you took advantage of an opportunity. *You took control.* You thwarted my defenses and my plans, and you sent TechX up in an ash cloud. Oh, yes, your clone here had attracted some attention by wearing an old hat. But it wasn't until you unleashed great destruction, until you showed that you *could* destroy, that things truly turned around for you. Because when people saw what you could do, they began to respect you. Some of them even began to *fear* you."

Fisher thought of Brody shrinking away from him in the gym.

"But what about friendship?" Dr. X went on in a mocking tone. "There are no friends, Fisher. Not really. There are only those who respect you, and those who don't. They either value what you can do for them, or they fear what you can do *to* them." He tapped a control, and the Fisher-bots lunged forward all at once. Fisher threw his arms up to protect himself, and the others all did the same, but another quick button push, and the bots stopped, stepping back into place.

"There, you see?" he said. "It's all about what you can do. Power. And it's about taking the chance to *seize* power. Opportunity."

He held out the control device to Fisher.

"Take it."

Fisher drew in a sharp breath.

"What?" he said, with a tremble in his voice.

"Take it," said Dr. X. "These bots aren't evil. They're just tools. They won't do anything that you don't tell them to. And that is the real point here. With them at your command, you can do *anything you want.*"

Fisher waited for Dr. X to pull his hand back, to laugh and command the Fisher-bots to attack. But he didn't. He extended the controller calmly to Fisher.

Fisher looked again at the bots. Was what Dr. X had said true? Was everything that had happened to him in the past month, all of the downs and ups, the defeats and the triumphs as simple as the shifting of power? Did people pay him attention only because he'd proven that he was dangerous?

He reached out and took the controller, and Dr. X let it go. Fisher looked down at its shining black surface, at its smooth inputs and soft-glowing displays. He thought of what he could do with such a force under his command. All of the wrongs he could right. What he could build.

What he would do.

Fisher raised his hand high above his head, and with a single, lightning-quick motion, hurled the controller against the hard tile floor, where it cracked, fell apart, and went dim.

"What . . . what did you *do* that for?!" Dr. X wailed, horrified. "What have you done?!" He threw himself to the floor, frantically trying to put the pieces of the controller back together.

The Fisher-bots powered off almost simultaneously.

Their heads drooped to their chests. Wally and FP ran excitedly around the deactivated bots, head-butting them and knocking them one by one to the ground.

"It's really very simple," Fisher said, crossing his arms in front of his chest, feeling like a newly crowned boxing champion. "You left out the most important thing about power. How much you have is important, I won't deny that. But what truly defines you isn't how much power you have. It's how you use it." He looked over and saw the pride radiating from Veronica's eyes. Any small doubts he'd had over whether he'd made the right choice were swept away. "*That* is why my friends care about me. Sure, lots of kids at Wompalog just think it's cool that I blew something up. But the people who know me stuck with me because of *why* I did it. To save my brother's life, and to keep you from taking over the world."

"Fisher . . . ," Alex said quietly.

Fisher held up a hand to hush his brother. "I'm not finished," he said, still staring at Dr. X. "My biggest mistake was thinking like you, Dr. X. I don't regret making Alex, but I made him for the wrong reasons. I wasn't solving any problems. I was running away from them. I tried to escape because I *could*. Because I had the power and the opportunity. I misused that power, and I've been paying for it ever since. We all have been.

"Before now I didn't really understand friendship. I

didn't think anyone actually cared about me. Now that I know that the world is more than just a power struggle, this all makes sense."

"Hey, Fisher?" Alex said again, more insistently.

"Hang on, I've got a little more to say," Fisher said. "Yes, I could do a lot of good with an army of androids at my command. But I did nothing to earn that power. I didn't create it, and I don't really understand it. And frankly, it's more power than any one person should hold."

As he finished his speech, he could almost imagine the rumbling of swollen applause from an invisible crowd.

*"Fisher!"* Alex said a third time. *"The floor is shaking."*

Fisher realized that the rumble was not in his head. He looked down and saw his shoelaces vibrating along with it.

"That controller must have been running all the traps and gadgets Three put around the school," said Amanda.

"Well," Fisher said, "in that case . . . let's leave. Really, really fast."

Amanda pulled the bound and groggy Three to his tied-up feet, put her shoulder into his stomach, and hoisted him into the air.

"You okay moving like that?" Alex said.

"We'll take turns," Amanda said, taking a deep breath. "Come on, let's go!"

Dr. X was on his knees, still mumbling into the remains

of the controller and sifting them through his fingers.

"Come on, Dr. X," Fisher said. "We have to go!"

Dr. X kept on mumbling, oblivious to the way the floor was bucking underneath them.

"Leave him!" Amanda shouted.

It was tempting. But Fisher wanted to see Dr. X brought to justice.

"Come on," Veronica said, sensing his hesitation. "You take one arm, I'll take the other."

Fisher was thankful Dr. X was such a scrawny man. Fisher and Veronica both hooked him under one arm and were able to pull him along easily, his heels dragging against the floor.

They dashed out of the science classroom and down the hall, ducking under another shower of extra-sharpened pencils. Amanda breathed heavily under the load she was carrying, stopping and starting as lockers blew open, sending textbooks as heavy as bricks flying through the air.

"Switch!" Alex said to the tiring Amanda, who put Three down just long enough for Alex to pick him up. Fisher waved everyone forward, nearly tripping over FP, who was scurrying along at his feet beside Einy and Berg. Then he realized Wally was gone.

"Where's Wally?" he shouted over a series of loud pops.

"Don't know!" Veronica said. "But there's no time to find him! Come on!"

Dr. X had finally realized that the building was coming apart around their ears, and had regained his feet. They had almost reached Wompalog's main hallway, the one that would lead them out of the danger zone, when hundreds of tiny red objects sprung down from the ceiling on thin wires, hanging menacingly in front of them.

"What are those?" said Amanda as they all skidded to a halt.

"Red pens," Fisher said, horrified.

They moved forward, the fumes from the countless felt-tip pens nearly suffocating them. Gagging and choking, Alex and Amanda dragged Three behind them. Dr. X clawed himself along in miserable silence.

"Come on, come on!" Fisher said, taking Veronica's arm when she stumbled. His head was swimming. As soon as they were clear of the pens, he took a deep breath and it began to clear. Amanda took her turn carrying Three again, and they made for the doors. Fisher's eyes streamed from the pen fumes and his lungs burned from running.

They were almost there . . . just another twenty feet . . .

Then an immense *thump* filled the hall as three giant spheres crashed down right in front of the doors, and began to roll toward them.

"Gym balls," Fisher said as another memory of Viking torture sprung up in his mind. These giant-sized gym

balls had been outfitted with steel-reinforced outer lay-
ers, armed in spikes, studs, and sickle blades. They were
rolling so fast, there was no way around them.

"In here, quick!" Alex shouted, kicking open the nearest classroom door. Fisher stood aside, letting Amanda
carry Three in first as the deadly balls picked up speed,
cutting up the floor in their path. Alex and Dr. X followed
next, then Fisher made sure Veronica was in before picking up FP and diving into the room.

The door had hardly closed before one of the deadly
spheres smashed into its frame. The booms and crashes
outside subsided, and Fisher pushed against the door,
which might as well have been a stone wall.

"Not budging," he said. "We'd need a bulldozer to get
out of here." He was going to say more when a sharp,
splintering sound cut him off.

"Look!" Alex said, pointing at the ceiling. Fisher
looked. A long crack had formed in the ceiling. The walls
started to shake.

"This place is about to come down," Amanda said, eyes
wide with panic. "We have to find another way out!"

Fisher immediately ran to the windows, but all of them
had steel shutters locked in place over them. They must
have been installed by Three's minions when he was forti-
fying the place. Everyone searched the walls and floor for
anything they could find—a vent, a trapdoor, even a weak

spot in the wall. But they came up empty. Every second, a new crack developed in the ceiling until it looked like a spider's web.

Alex and Fisher took turns slamming the metal shutters with chairs, trying to break through them. Fisher's eyes stung with sweat, and his arms were exhausted. Suddenly, Veronica wrenched him backward, away from the windows.

"The wall," she said, "it's coming down!"

A loud buzzing sound filled the air, and a spray of dust hit the group as long lines appeared in the plaster beneath the windows.

Straight lines. *Perfectly* straight lines.

"It's not breaking," Fisher said excitedly. "It's being cut!"

A neat four-foot square of wall fell away, revealing the outside world. A tall, strong-jawed man in a suit stood outside.

"Agent Mason!" Fisher cried out.

"Nice to see you, boys," said FBI Special Agent Syd Mason as he and the two saw-wielding agents with him backed away from the school. "Now come on out of there before the whole place comes down."

Fisher let Alex, who'd picked up Three, go first, Amanda by his side. Dr. X shuffled out next, with Einy and Berg at his feet, and Fisher helped Veronica through the hole before casting one last look at the crumbling school, taking FP under his arm, and following her out.

The room's ceiling fell a few seconds later, and thick dust clouds puffed into the air as other parts of the school caved in, leaving Wompalog in ruins.

"Agggh!" Dr. X screamed, collapsing to his knees and watching the dust plume rise. "Can you do nothing but destroy?? Demolish? Every time I come close to my true destiny, you make it crumble into powder! It's all gone. . . ." He keeled over into a fetal position, hugging his knees to his chest. "It's all gone."

"Agent Mason," said Fisher, "allow me to present Mr. Harold Granger, also known as Dr. X."

"Yes," said Mason. "We've been pursuing him for quite some time. Certain things he let slip on *Family Feudalism* convinced us we had our man. I also heard that my inside man on the show uncovered some very unusual machinery hooked into the broadcast equipment. It's been disabled."

"Good," Amanda said. "That's what's been making everyone crazy."

"I figured as much," said Mason.

"What about our parents?" said Alex, half terrified. "Are they okay?"

"They're just fine," said Mason. "I had one of my agents check your place while I headed here. Your home is fine."

He smiled. "You just might have some gridlock for a while. A hundred thirty-five robots are collapsed in the street. We've got major cleanup crews on the way, but even they may have their hands full."

Fisher felt like his knees had turned to string cheese. Alex almost shook with relief.

"How'd you find us?" said Alex.

"Our little friend here," Mason said, and Fisher realized that Wally was standing next to him, looking pleased with himself. "We had the whole neighborhood under surveillance. He came and found me and led us back to school. From there, we used high-power microphones to pick up your voices inside and pinpoint your positions."

Dr. X was still mumbling to himself as the other agents cuffed him, dragged him to his feet, and led him away. Einy and Berg had scampered off in the direction of the baseball field once the agents had approached. Fisher figured they would be just fine fending for themselves.

"*This,*" said Alex, pointing at Three, who lay on the ground, blank faced and silent as a glacier, "is the one responsible for everything that's gone wrong in the past few days."

"I see," said Mason, frowning. "Well . . . I'm not sure how he'll be handled, legally. He's not an adult, after all. And technically he doesn't exist . . . but I'm sure we'll find some punishment appropriate for him." For one second, his kind face flashed with grim determination. Fisher was glad he wasn't on Agent Mason's bad side.

Mason hauled Three to his feet.

"What do you have to say to that?" Fisher couldn't help but gloating.

"Nothing," Three said simply. "Talking is a waste of energy at this point. It will not increase my chance of escape. But I do have one final thing to say to you."

Fisher forced himself to meet Three's pitiless gaze. Veronica came to his side, putting an arm around his shoulders.

"When Dr. X modified your genetic sequence to create me, he did not have to add anything," Three said, with a humorless smile. "He did not have to modify anything, either. All he had to do was remove a few things. A few emotional buffers, perhaps. Some moral codes."

Fisher felt a shiver go up his spine as Three leaned in.

"Do you see, Fisher? *Everything that I am is within you. We are the same.*" His eyes were black as a tunnel. "You will carry me with you for the rest of your life, inches from the surface. You will go to sleep every night hoping that I won't wake up inside of you by morning. Good-bye, Fisher."

"That's enough," Agent Mason said gruffly. "You've had your say." And he led Three to the car where the other agents were waiting with Dr. X.

W = Time it will take to rebuild Wompalog Middle School in days

$$\frac{d_f + d_s}{c} + p + f + h = W$$

let:

$d_f$ = days repairing foundation

$d_s$ = days rebuilding structure

$c$ = construction delays

$p$ = days painting

$f$ = days installing flooring

$h$ = days installing HVAC*

*survey and map out new air duct plan?

# WHO CARES!? NO SCHOOL

$$\frac{d_f + d_s}{c} + p + f + h = 114.0179$$

"I'm sorry, Fisher," Veronica said quietly. "Please don't worry too much about what he said."

"I won't," said Fisher. "What he said is true for everyone. We've all got a Three in us somewhere. We're all capable of using our talents for selfish gains and destruction. The more power you have, the more responsibility you have to use it properly."

"Why, Fisher," Veronica said, "that's exactly what I was about to say to you. You may have a better grasp on human interaction than you think."

He laughed. "Maybe. My learning curve has just been a little . . . steeper," he said, gesturing to the mostly destroyed middle school. "Let's hope the rest of my education doesn't involve so many robot armies. Colleges aren't going to accept me if they expect their campus to turn into the apocalypse in the middle of my sophomore year."

Alex and Amanda walked up, hand in hand. FP trotted in happy circles around them.

"Okay," Amanda said. "You blew up the school. What now?"

"Pizza," Fisher said promptly. "I'm starving. That work for all of you?" Amanda, Veronica, and Alex beamed. Alex let go of Amanda's hand to give Fisher a hug. Fisher clapped his new brother on the back, noting how well a hug works between people of exactly the same size and shape. Veronica and Amanda hugged next to them, laughing happily.

Sirens cut through their celebration, and Mason shouted to them from his unmarked black sedan.

"Sounds like your antics attracted some attention!" he said, nodding toward the sound of the sirens. "I'm sure you could spend a few hours at the station explaining everything that happened to the police, but it might be easier just to vanish." And he winked.

"We were just leaving," Fisher said. "Thanks for everything, Agent Mason!"

"Call me Syd! And don't worry, once we process these two, we'll make sure the cops are up to speed about everything. Well . . . maybe not *everything*," he said, with a wink at Alex. "Take care, all of you!"

The FBI agents drove off with Dr. X and Three crammed into the back of their car.

Veronica took Fisher's hand, and little electric bolts raced up his arm. They walked off, FP at his heels and Alex and Amanda beside them, and Fisher breathed easily for what felt like the first time in weeks.

# ≋ CHAPTER 21 ≋

I destroyed TechX and I was cool for a few weeks.
I destroyed our school and I became a Wompalog legend.
—Fisher Bas, Personal Notes

"Part of me's waiting for all of these people to start World War Three because of a dispute over spicy fries or something," said Amanda.

In the two weeks since Wompalog's collapse, the school had brought in trailers to serve as temporary classrooms, but the school's parking lot wasn't big enough to hold them. The only establishment whose lot *did* have the space to accommodate fifty tractor trailers was the King of Hollywood on the former TechX site, which had graciously offered the school use of its parking lot.

Suddenly, getting lunch at school wasn't the daily parade of horrors that it used to be. There were whispered rumors that the rebuilding of the school would include updating and improving the cafeteria, but nobody wanted to get their hopes up too high.

Fisher, Alex, Amanda, and Veronica sat around a table at the King of Hollywood. Fisher smiled across the table at Alex. It felt good to relax and not be checking every shadow for a new and monstrous threat to all humanity.

"Don't worry, the subliminal signal's gone," he said. "Agent Mason said it was basically sending Morse code directly to the brain during episodes of *Family Feudalism*. It was literally rewriting people's behavior. Even machines could pick up the pulses as information packets, which had the same effect."

Veronica smiled. "Now reality TV can go back to destroying society in the less literal way."

FP was curled up next to Fisher's chair, half sleeping, half chewing his way through a quadruple Kingburger the size of a basketball. As soon as Fisher and FP had arrived, the KOH's manager had given it to Fisher "on the house." FP's reputation was starting to precede him, especially after the Rainforest Cafe incident.

"Heard what they're saying about Wompalog?" said Amanda, sipping at a massive soda. "It could take up to five or six months to repair the damage and inspect the whole building for safety."

"Three really rigged the place up," said Alex, leaning back in his chair and letting the front legs come up off the ground. "He must have worked all night every night for weeks, with dozens of Fisher-bots to help him. I don't mind the trailers, though."

"Hey!" said Ms. Snapper, walking up. She had to peek over the pile of spicy star fries on her tray. "Nice to see you all having a good time. What did you think of the experiment we did in bio this morning?"

"Well," Amanda said, "using spicy sauce as the food source to grow a bacterial colony might put me off those star fries for a while, but it was pretty cool."

"They must make that stuff with alchemy," Fisher said, nodding to the tub of special sauce on Ms. Snapper's tray. "I was never able to reproduce it, even in a lab."

"Well, I'm just relieved they got that fiend Dr. X," said Ms. Snapper. "But I can't believe he turned out to be Mr. Granger! I didn't know him very well when he was at the school, but even so. It was bizarre when he just popped up on that show after disappearing from Wompalog, and I guess that was pretty suspicious. Still . . ."

"I'm just happy to see him behind bars," said Fisher.

For now the truth about Three would remain with them. The FBI had released news of Dr. X's capture. Everyone had seen him appear as Harold Granger on *Family Feudalism*, so his secret identity was now blown. It wasn't difficult convincing the public that an already feared mastermind like him had been responsible for recent events. The official story was that Three had just been the head android, sending messages out in Dr. X's place to mask who was really in charge. Given the way Three spoke, making him out to be a robot wasn't too tough a sell.

"I'll let you get back to your food," Ms. Snapper said, smiling. "See you tomorrow!"

Fisher turned to Veronica as their teacher walked away.

"Are you sure you're all right with keeping the truth about Three to ourselves for a little while?" he said, glancing across the table at Alex with a little twinge of guilt. Secrets had caused an awful lot of trouble lately.

"Yes," Veronica said, after just a second's hesitation. "In the aftermath, it's more important to fix the damage, rebuild, and regroup. So long as we reveal the whole truth when the time is right."

"Absolutely," Amanda said, putting her hand down in the center of the table. Alex put his on hers, Fisher put his on Alex's, and Veronica put hers on his.

"When the time is right, the truth," said Alex, and everyone else nodded.

"The truth," they echoed. Fisher felt an extra little brush from Veronica's thumb as they withdrew their hands, and his heart did a brief tap dance routine around his rib cage.

"Hey, kids," said a man in a sharply tailored gray suit and mirrored sunglasses, striding up to the table with a wombat by his side.

"Agent Mason!" the kids cried simultaneously.

They'd learned that Agent Mason had followed Dr. X

to Palo Alto. Wally's performance at the Rainforest Cafe hadn't been a coincidence at all. Mason had sent the wombat in to scout ahead before he arrived. He'd been operating under absolute secrecy, undercover, posing as one of Harold Granger's fans, which was why they'd never heard back from him.

All along, he'd been keeping watch on the kids—and on Wally. But he'd had to wait until the last moment to reveal himself. If he hadn't, Three might have hunted him down and eliminated him before he could act.

"Is everything all right?" Fisher said. "Are Dr. X and Three secure?"

"Very secure," said Mason, taking off his shades and smiling. "We added a maximum-security, solitary wing to a juvenile hall for Three. We're trying to find a way to bring him back into society somehow, but . . . it's a little challenging. I'm sure we'll think of something. And speaking of rejoining society . . ." He gave Wally a scratch around the ears. "Our little friend here may still be quick and bright eyed, but in wombat years, he's due to retire. I'd take him in myself, but I have to travel so much for work that I don't think I could take proper care of him." He smiled at Amanda.

"Ms. Cantrell, I would be honored if you would care to take in Wally for some long overdue R & R."

"I'd be happy to, Agent Mason," Amanda said, smiling

down at Wally. "It's the least I can do to thank him."

"Agent Mason," Alex said, with a gleam of powerful gratitude in his eyes, "thanks. You could've made life really difficult for me and you didn't."

"The only people who deserve difficult lives," said Mason, slipping his sunglasses back on, "are those who make life difficult for others. Take care, kids. I've no doubt I'll see you again."

Fisher watched Mason walk away. He hoped that the next time they saw him would be for a victory party, and not because Dr. X's dancing whales had developed higher consciousness and opposable thumbs.

Then he looked down and saw Wally nudging FP awake. FP was so excited to see his furry friend that he started to chase him around the table.

"Okay, FP," Fisher said as the chase got faster. "Take it easy, boy. . . ."

"Come on, Wally," Amanda said. "Slow down a little!"

Ignoring Fisher completely, FP chased Wally up onto the counter. Wally, being smarter than the average wombat, took cover behind an open cash register, and FP didn't even slow down. FP landed with a crash in the paper tray. Dollar bills started flying, and customers ducked and shrieked.

Fisher sighed.

From cloning himself, to seeing his clone become

popular, to blowing up TechX, to pursuing his clone to LA and fighting robotic dinosaurs, to saving the town from Three . . . it had been quite a start to the school year. But if he could get through the seventh grade, he could do anything.

Alex and Amanda were already chasing after the two balls of mayhem.

"Fisher!" Alex called as FP chased Wally past the condiments and sent a spray of mustard across the room. "A little help?"

"I'll be right back," he said to Veronica.

"I'll be right here," she said, and squeezed his hand and smiled.

I did something pretty crazy. I lived in a world that didn't even want one of me, and I gave it two. My selfishness nearly brought that number back to zero. But I discovered a couple of things. You mean more to the world than you think, and it's never too late to learn from yourself.

# ACKNOWLEDGMENTS

Clone 3! Clone 3! When I heard that I would get to write the then-untitled third Clone book, I was extremely happy to get to explore what I've come to call the Cloniverse in greater depth. I actually slipped the name *Game of Clones* into a long list of suggestions, hoping they'd spot it and pick it out of the crowd as a favorite. Naturally, they did, and here we are.

Thanks must go out to all the usual suspects, of course. Lauren and Lexa at Paper Lantern for unearthing me in the first place, dusting me off, and putting me on their specimen shelf. Beth, with whom I worked closely and has now moved onward to greater things. And, of course, Greg, for his vast editing prowess and truly spiffy eyeglasses. To all of my family and friends, you are wholly responsible for my continued sanity. So if I snap and run off into the woods and spend all day talking to dirt and painting trees blue, it's your fault. No pressure.

Finally, thank you to the people who stole my previous computer out of my bedroom for waiting until this book was mostly done and everything was backed up in multiple places. I hope whoever owns that machine now is unaware of its felonious origin and is using it to better humankind and send us to the stars.

Turn the page for a peek at the hilarious and fun-filled
*We Clone in Peace*

# CLONES
## vs.
# Aliens

### THE CLONE CHRONICLES #4

Available in hardcover and eBook from
Egmont Publishing in Spring 2015

I walked into school one morning and destroyed a math test. I walked into school the next day and destroyed the school.                        —Fisher Bas, Journal

"One . . . more . . . piece . . . ," Fisher Bas said. Sweat beaded on his forehead. His breathing slowed to near hibernation levels, his hand shifted tremblingly into place. It was Friday afternoon, the end of the school week, and most kids were already on their way home. He, however, had one task left. An outdoor project of unprecedented scope. He was a single piece away from completing what was without a doubt his greatest feat of engineering.

*Click.*

With the gentle sound of a final, perfect connection slotting home, it was done. Fisher stepped back carefully, shading his eyes against the sun. It truly was a wonder of geometric achievement, a proud symbol of humanity's eternal struggle against gravity.

It was the world's largest freestanding structure built entirely out of King of Hollywood Spicy Star Fry boxes— and would, Fisher hoped, serve as the basis for Wompalog's most impressive Thanksgiving float.

"It's beautiful," breathed Alex, Fisher's clone. Or, to be more specific, his first and least evil clone.

Two weeks earlier, Fisher's second and *very* evil clone, Three, had attempted to take over the city with an army of androids that all looked identical to Fisher. He had very nearly succeeded. In the final showdown, the Wompalog school building had been utterly wrecked. So for now, school was a bunch of trailers hauled into the massive parking lot surrounding the King of Hollywood—which meant constant access to the mind-numbingly delicious fries, and lots of time during lunch to fiddle around with their packaging.

For the first time in a long time, Fisher was relaxed. Thanksgiving was next week. And better, Dr. X was in jail. Three was in the most secure custody the FBI could arrange for minors. Veronica was happy with him. And Alex was his own person instead of a dark secret.

Fisher and Alex had been through an awful lot together in the few short months of Alex's life, whether saving the world from Dr. X, freeing Palo Alto from Three's clutches, or devising a method to trick their dad's genetically engineered cookie-sniffing mongoose when she came into Fisher's room unannounced.

Unless something fell out of the sky in the next few days, then finally, *finally,* Fisher could take it easy for a little while.

Fisher's ears perked up.

"Do you hear something?" he said to Alex.

"Like what?" Alex said.

"Like a hiss, or a whine, or a . . . " Fisher turned, horrified. *Oh, no.* " . . . squeal."

With a resounding oink, a fuzzy, pointy-eared pink missile careened right through Fisher's fry box tower and into Fisher's arms. Fisher tumbled backward with such force he crashed into Alex, and the three of them—boys and pig—sank into the pile of toppled boxes.

Flying Pig, Alex and Fisher's pet, was a loyal and lovable creature who also seemed to be, aside from a black hole or a gamma ray burst, the single most destructive force in the universe.

After a minute or two of awkward clawing, Fisher's head finally breached the surface of the cooking oil-scented heap.

"Tell me you at least got a picture," he said to Alex. "That was a week of work."

Alex's arm popped up from beneath the cardboard tide, phone clutched in his fist.

"Thank Higgs," Fisher said, hauling Alex out of the wreckage of his masterpiece. "I would've had to reassemble it with glue before mounting it on the float, anyway. The important thing is that we've got the photo to guide us."

FP emerged from the pile a few seconds later, a

# Plans for
# Spicy Fry Box
# Parade Float

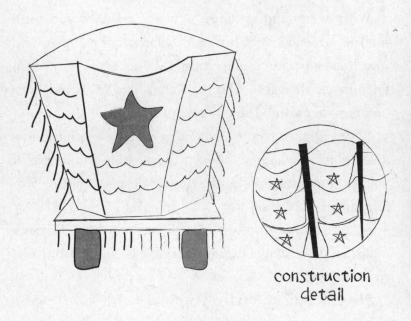

construction
detail

grease-stained box hanging from each ear.

"It's two thirty," Alex said, dusting the oily remains of fry residue from his shoulder. "Time to head home. Maximizing our time away from Wompalog would be optimal."

"I know," Fisher said. "I wrote the equation."

The pleasant residential area Fisher and Alex passed through on the way home showed barely any indication that it had, briefly, been the victim of a hostile android takeover. FP sniffed happily at well-maintained hedges. There weren't any scorch marks or car wrecks, no burned gears or other robotic debris. It looked like any other ordinary neighborhood, where decent people led happy lives and did not have to deal with mechanical armies commanded by under-five-foot tyrant clones.

Fisher breathed easily, hoping it would stay that way at least until the new year. That didn't seem like so much to ask, really.

At the end of their short walk, the Bas home came into view. It was, in fact, very difficult to miss. A cluster of antennae sprang from the roof, transmitting, receiving, and collecting data from dozens of experiments. Mrs. Bas's garden was visible from more than a block away, mostly because of the massive cornstalk that jutted higher than the house. Mr. Bas had named it Fee, as in Fi Fo Fum.

"Tomorrow's going to be fantastic," Fisher said. "Loopity Land will be the biggest thing in town since the first King of Hollywood opened."

"I'm still shocked that our parents helped design an amusement park," Alex said. "I mean, I could see Dad putting together a roller coaster for marmosets or flatworms or something, but entertaining *people*? New territory."

"It's true," Fisher said thoughtfully. The Bas's Liquid

Door front gate, as dense as lead when sitting idle, reduced itself to a vapor-like state as it recognized Alex and Fisher's DNA, allowing them to pass through. "Our parents might be geniuses, but their social skills are definitely remedial."

Mr. and Mrs. Bas had announced earlier in the week that they had secretly been working for over a year on a vast amusement park that was at last nearing completion. Tomorrow, Saturday, would be a trial run to which only the designers and builders were invited.

Fisher, however, had other plans. He'd engineered a special hovering pickpocket drone. If it worked correctly, it would secretly float up behind his parents after they'd entered the park, slip the special entrance passes from their pockets, and deliver them right back to Fisher.

"We're home!" Alex said as he pushed open the front door, which didn't change shape or scan people for DNA because it was just a regular door made of wood. *No need to reinvent the wheel*, Mrs. Bas always said—which was a slightly confused philosophy, since she had, in fact, reinvented the wheel. Three times.

"Hey, boys!" their dad said from the landing halfway down the stairs. "Welcome ho-oooooooooo—" He was interrupted mid-greeting by one of his more recent genetic experiments, Paul, the walking octopus, who had just wrapped himself around Mr. Bas's ankles. Paul had lungs as well as gills, and two extra tentacles that were strong enough to let him glide around on the floor.

With a loud *thunk*, Mr. Bas and Paul landed in a tangled heap at the bottom of the stairs. Paul's tentacles waved in panic as he wiggled underneath Mr. Bas. Fisher was grateful he had recently installed shock-absorbing, impact-reducing stairs. Living with his parents, and his dad in particular, had made them an obvious invention to pursue.

Walter Bas rolled over so Paul could slip out from underneath him. The good-natured cephalopod freed himself, shaking his tentacles out and rubbing his bulbous head. FP stepped up and sniffed at Paul curiously. He was still getting used to having the strange animal around. Paul gave FP a little pat on the snout, and the pig gave a friendly snort.

"Getting into the roller coaster spirit a little early, huh?" said Alex, helping their dad up.

"I guess I am," Mr. Bas said, chuckling a little as he straightened up. "Tomorrow's the big day!"

"I can't wait to see it," Fisher said, feeling the gentle pressure of Paul's many-armed hello on his left calf.

"Unfortunately, you'll have to, at least for a little bit," Mr. Bas said sternly, adjusting his glasses on his nose. Fisher felt Alex's sideways look. "There are a lot of things we need to test before the park can open to visitors," Mr.

Bas went on. "We won't be certain everything is safe and working properly until at least a week of trials have been done. *Especially* on the M3."

Fisher's heart skipped. The M3. Short for Mega Mars Madness. Soon to be the greatest roller coaster in existence. His parents had finally relented and showed Fisher the architectural plans they'd drawn up for its completion. The M3 was so complex even Fisher didn't fully understand it. All he knew was that the beauty of the physics of it overwhelmed him.

Fisher had never been on a roller coaster before; he'd always been too scared. But no more. Maybe it was the influence Alex had had on him. Fisher was still scared, there was no doubt about it. He was just less willing to let fear stop him.

"Of course, we understand," Fisher said, smiling nervously and nudging Alex with an elbow. "We can be patient. It's only a week, after all."

"Boys! I had no idea you were home. Is it three o'clock already? I haven't even had lunch," said Mrs. Bas, stepping in from the living room with a small beaker in her hand. She tapped the beaker a couple of times with a fingernail. "You know how time flies when I'm working on something. Well, I'd better get back to testing this project."

"What is it?" asked Fisher, stepping forward to get a better look. But it just looked like a beaker full of water.

8

"I call it H2Info," she said. "Scientists have talked about the idea of storing information in liquid form for years. But I imagined going a step further. What if, instead of just storing information as a liquid and then putting the liquid in a machine that could read it like a disk, you cut out the middle step? What if you could ingest the liquid and have the information transferred directly to your mind?" She shook the beaker slightly. "There are millions of nanomachines in here . . . tiny drones that can interpret the information coded into the water molecules and create new neural pathways . . . literally writing information into the brain."

"Wow," Fisher said. "What's in this one?"

"'Baa Baa Black Sheep' in Russian," she said, looking a little sheepish. "I needed something that simple for this first test. I'm going to call a physicist friend in Saint Petersburg and see how I do. Wish me luck!" With that, she tossed back the liquid and walked upstairs, already humming the rhyme.

"I'd better put this little guy back in his tank and get back to work," Mr. Bas said, patting Paul on the head and scooping him into his arms before heading up himself.

"They don't suspect a thing," Fisher said, smiling at his brother as FP hopped around their feet. "We'll have to keep a low profile tomorrow, but since the park is so big and there are only two of us—"

A chime sounded at a control panel in the hall. Somebody was at the gate. Alex quickly tapped the button to manually mist-ify the Liquid Door without bothering to ask the house who it was.

"Uh, yeah," Alex said, "about that . . . " He opened the door.

Amanda Cantrell stood on the step, black hair shimmering, glasses gleaming in the sun.

"Hey," she said.

"Hey," Alex replied, glancing nervously over his shoulder at Fisher.

She glanced over her own shoulder, as if worried someone had followed her. "You got it?" she said, dropping her voice to a whisper.

"I got it," Alex said.

"It?" Fisher said. "What is 'it'?" He crossed his arms.

Alex reached into his backpack and pulled out a small plastic card.

"Wait a minute, wait a minute," Fisher said, rushing forward and snatching it from Alex's hand. "Is that one of our parents' Loopity Land passes? We can't steal them before *they* need them or they'll find out, that's the whole reason I made the pickpocket drone! Besides, *we* were going to use the passes."

Alex gave Fisher a very large, very fake smile, reached into his backpack again, and pulled out a whole sheaf of the specially encrypted entrance cards. Amanda quickly tucked them into her own bag.

"I didn't steal them," Alex said. "Or, well, I did steal one, briefly. I figured out how to duplicate them. With CURTIS's help."

Fisher's eye started to twitch, and he fought down a surge of irritation. How could Alex have plotted with Amanda behind Fisher's back when Fisher had trusted him to plot with Fisher behind their parents' backs!

"Let me get this straight," Fisher said in a harsh whisper. "You conspired with my artificial intelligence behind my back to make counterfeit tickets. You're going to flood the park with kids, and people will find out, and then—"

"I made one for Veronica, too," Alex interjected.

At the mention of Veronica Greenwich, Fisher's objections got into a pileup somewhere between his soft palate and his teeth, realized they weren't needed anymore, and retreated back down his throat.

" . . . Okay," Fisher said after a minute. His cheeks felt like he had Bunsen burners under them. Amanda smirked.

"Glad that's settled," Alex said. "Don't worry, Fisher. It's a big park, and we'll make sure the kids keep a low profile. Besides, I engineered the passes to self-destruct after use so they can't be traced back to us. All our friends agreed that if they get caught by security, they'll claim to have snuck in."

"Good thinking," Fisher said, ignoring the anxiety that resurged after Alex said *all our friends* and wondering if it was sad that the mere thought of his dream girl could defeat him so easily. He could take on evil robots, evil clones, and evil mad scientists, but the thought of one single, beautiful girl stopped Fisher's brain right in its tracks.

Sharing the brand-new Loopity Land with Veronica wasn't a chance Fisher could ever have passed up—Alex knew him too well. Even with things so good between Veronica and him, Fisher was still just beginning to figure out how to act around her and what made her happy. It wasn't as straightforward as relativity or advanced particle physics. Loopity Land was a risk, but one well worth taking. Besides, how wrong could things possibly go?